rhymes with witches

Also by Lauren Myracle

ttyl
Eleven
Kissing Kate

rhymes with witches

Lauren Myracle

Amulet Books
New York

Library of Congress Cataloging-in-Publication Data:

Myracle, Lauren, 1969-

Rhymes with witches / Lauren Myracle.

p. cm.

Summary: High school freshman Jane believes that she would do anything
to be popular until she is selected to be in the school's most exclusive
clique and learns that popularity has a price.

hardcover ISBN 0-8109-5859-7

paperback ISBN 13: 978-0-8109-9215-3

paperback ISBN 10: 0-8109-9215-9

[1. Popularity—Fiction. 2. Cliques (Sociology)—Fiction. 3. Witchcraft—Fiction. 4. Conduct
of life—Fiction. 5. Interpersonal relations—Fiction. 6. High schools—Fiction. 7. Schools—Fiction.]

I. Title.

PZ7.M9955Rh 2005

[Fic]—dc22

2004023447

Originaly published in hardcover by Amulet Books in 2005

Copyright © 2006 Lauren Myracle

Printed in U.S.A.

3   5   7   9   10   8   6   4   2

Designed by Jay Colvin

HNA

harry n. abrams, inc.

a subsidiary of La Martinière Groupe

115 West 18th Street

New York, NY 10011

www.hnabooks.com

For Laura,
the original Bitch,
who couldn't be a bitch if she tried

Acknowledgments

Thanks to Tobin Anderson for inducting me into the world of the weird. Thanks to Laura Pritchett, Todd Mitchell, and Jack Martin for helping me make the weird even weirder. And thanks times ten to Susan Van Metre, who tempered weirdness with vulnerability, spookiness with humanity. Susan, you are the cat's meow.

beg

I so shouldn't have worn this thong. It was hiking up my butt, and there was nothing I could do about it because there was no way to subtly reach up and yank it out. "They're comfortable," Mom had said. Then, "Well, they do take some getting used to. But Jane, if you don't want panty lines . . ."

Thanks, Mom. This was the wedgie from hell.

"I'm thinking maybe board shorts and a red tank top," Alicia said.

I shifted on the hard cafeteria chair. My new dress, the one that demanded no panty lines, wrinkled under my thighs.

"*If* I can find black board shorts," Alicia went on. "Or board shorts with enough black in them to count as black. We all have to wear black and red, did I tell you?"

"Go Devils," I said.

Alicia speared a spaghetti noodle. She twirled it around her fork. "You're being stupid, you know. They have spots for five freshmen. You could sign up after lunch and still have—"

She was interrupted by a high-pitched yowl as a rangy butterscotch-colored cat bolted from the kitchen. It leaped over one table and skidded down another, sending a plate of spaghetti crashing to the floor. Cries erupted as people jerked out of its way. Chairs screeched.

"Get out! Get *out*!" one of the cafeteria ladies shrieked, brandishing a spatula. "Filthy overgrown rodent!"

The cat bounded through the wide double doors. The cafeteria lady flung her spatula, and the cat jumped sideways and tore down the hall.

"And *stay* out!" the cafeteria lady yelled. She stared after it, her face flushed and her hairnet slipping out of place. She stomped back to the kitchen to the applause of the student body.

"Jesus Christ," Alicia said. "You'd think we could have one day—*one* day—without those cats breaking a frickin' plate. But nooo. The whole damn school is possessed, I'm not even kidding."

"They're cats, Alicia. Not spinning-head girls from *The Exorcist*."

"They're diseased. Why doesn't someone call the Humane Society?"

I raised my eyebrows. Mr. Van Housen, the principal, *had* called the Humane Society, as well as Animal Control. He'd sent out e-mail after e-mail explaining the difficulty of capturing feral cats once they've taken over a given territory, e-mails that Alicia had received along with everyone else.

"Whatever," she said. "But it's driving me insane." She stabbed a fresh noodle and demanded, "So will you? Sign up after lunch?"

"I'm not trying out for cheerleading," I said.

"But *why*? I know you're convinced you're this big loser, but you could at least try out."

My skin grew warm. "I'm not convinced I'm a loser. Who said I'm convinced I'm a loser?"

"Hmm. Would that possibly be you, Jane?" She assumed a hangdog expression. "'I am worthless and alone because my daddy abandoned me. Boo-hoo-hoo.'"

I put down my garlic bread. Alicia was not nearly as clever as she liked to think she was.

"I'm kidding," she said. Her face showed her regret, although only for an instant. Being real with each other wasn't something Alicia and I knew how to do very well. "But how are you going to, like, rise above it if you never even make the effort? I'm serious. Don't you ever just want to be more than who you are?"

A new disruption sent ripples through the crowded cafeteria, saving me from having to answer. It was the Bitches, Crestview's elite, strolling majestically through the doors. They filed in according to rank: first Keisha, who was a senior; then Bitsy, a junior; then Mary Bryan, a sophomore. A lull fell in the hum of eating and talking, and then conversations swelled back up. Brad Johnson's laugh rang out, shouting, *Look at me! Look at me!*

Sukie Karing smiled hard and waved. "Over here!" she called. "I saved you guys seats!"

"*They're* not cheerleaders," I said. "You don't have to be a cheerleader to be cool."

Alicia snorted. Still, she straightened her spine as Bitsy passed. So aware, all of us, of being in their presence. I watched as they waltzed into the food line, then I gloomily regarded my spaghetti, knowing they'd emerge with fettuccine alfredo.

Alicia sagged into her usual slump. "That's because they're beyond cheerleader-cool," she said. "The usual rules don't apply."

"Well, that's not fair," I said. But it was a half-hearted complaint, because to complain about something, you had to not like that thing, and I liked the Bitches as much as anyone. Liked them—ha. Craved them, yearned for them, wanted to be them. Bought this stupid dress to impress them, for god's sake, not that they'd ever notice. So really, the complaint was less about them and more about me.

Keisha walked out of the food line with her loaded tray, and Tommy Arnez quoted loudly from *Casablanca*.

"I came for the waters!" he cried. He and Curtis MacKeen started a *Casablanca* riff, their voices growing louder and their Bogart impressions heavier, and Keisha rewarded them with a smile.

"So will you at least come watch next Monday, when we do our official auditions?" Alicia asked. "I need someone to cheer me on."

I turned back to her. "I thought the cheering was your job."

She scowled, *Oh aren't you funny.*

"Of course I'll come," I said. "I'll clap like crazy."

Keisha, Bitsy, and Mary Bryan dropped down by Sukie Karing, and Mary Bryan tore open a packet of cheese and sprinkled it onto her carbonara. Not fettuccine alfredo, but carbonara. I could see the pancetta.

"I just hope I can do a split by then," Alicia said. "I am so inflexible it's not even funny." Her eyes drifted to the Bitches, then made their way back to me. She sucked on her Diet Coke. "So what's *your* big news? Before homeroom you said you had something to tell me."

"I did?" I said. "Huh. I can't remember."

"Liar," she said. "Did it have to do with your dad? I bet it did, didn't it? Did he send you another dippy gift?"

As a matter of fact, he had. He'd mailed me a souvenir from Egypt, the latest stop on his quest to find himself. I wadded up my napkin.

"Because you really can tell me," she said. "I won't say anything mean. I promise."

"I've got to go," I said. I tossed my napkin on my tray and stood up. "I've got to finish my Spanish."

"Nerd," she said.

"Spaz," I said.

I slung my backpack over my shoulder. A lump in the bottom bumped my hip. I took my tray to the conveyor belt, then headed past Mary Bryan and Keisha and Bitsy toward the door. *Easy now,* I told myself. Stomach in. Chin up. Expression alert, indicating rich inner life. Three, two, one—smile!

Oh god, did I have oregano stuck in my teeth?

Mary Bryan smiled back at me. At *me.* At easy, breezy me. I floated out of the room as my thong climbed up my butt.

🐈

During Spanish, I reached into my backpack and closed my hand around Dad's present. A small brown teddy bear, just right for an eleven-year-old, wearing a shirt that read I LOVE CAIRO.

🐈

"We've got spirit, yes we do! We've got spirit—how 'bout you?"

Whoops and cheers assaulted me as I walked across campus after class. Clusters of freshman girls, each group with their own senior leader, bounced and leaped and yelled. I searched for Alicia and spotted her on the courtyard of Askew Hall. With her pale skin and inky black hair, she was an easy target. The other girls were doing a step-cross-step kind of movement, but Alicia crossed when they stepped and stepped when they crossed. Her tongue jammed against her lower lip, making it bulge. She did that when she concentrated.

She rammed the girl beside her, and my face heated up for no good reason. It wasn't me who had rammed Chelsea Olsen. It wasn't me who appeared to be nursing a wad of chew.

Stop it, I scolded myself. *Be nice.* With Alicia, I was always trying to be a better friend than I was.

Footsteps clipped behind me, and I turned to see a breathless

Mary Bryan. Mary Bryan! Her cheeks were pink and her honey-blond hair was slipping from her ponytail. Her striped T-shirt stopped above her belly button, revealing an inch of tummy above her low-slung jeans.

"Jane," she said. "Hey! I was looking for you."

I glanced behind me, even though she'd said my name as clear as could be. "You were?"

"Where are you headed? I'll walk with you."

"Uh, I'm just going to the library. I have a report due for English." This wasn't true. Really I was just going to hide out until three when Mom picked me up. I would hole up in one of the carrels and reread the Ramona books I loved back in sixth grade.

"Ugh," Mary Bryan groaned. "Hate English reports. My last one was on that play *Pygmalion*, which, I'm sorry, totally sucked."

"That's the one with the 'Rain in Spain' song, right?" I asked. My nerves made me blabber. "Where that professor—what was his name? Oh yeah, Henry Huggins. And he turns a street urchin into a lady and then falls in love with her?"

Mary Bryan's lips came together, and my stupidity hit me like a blow. Mary Bryan was a sophomore. She'd never said more than "hi" to me, and now, when she did, I gave a show-offy speech about a play she probably hadn't even finished.

"Close," she said, "only you're thinking of the musical, which is *My Fair Lady*. In the play, they don't fall in love."

"Oh."

"And it's Henry Higgins, not Huggins," Mary Bryan said. "For what it's worth." Idly, she dipped one finger under the waist of her jeans and scratched her tummy. "Anyway . . . you want to hang out sometime?"

Her words barely made it past my embarrassment. And when they did, they made no sense. Again I swiveled my head to see who she was really talking to.

"Gooooo, team!" the wannabe cheerleaders cried.

"Team!" echoed Alicia, one beat late.

"Um," I said. My brain was jammed. "Um . . ."

"I'll call you," Mary Bryan said. She checked out the cheer-leading girls, who pinwheeled their arms and flung themselves in the air. Her eyebrows edged higher as Alicia landed wrong on her ankle. "Shit!" Alicia cried, audible even from here.

Mary Bryan pulled out of it. "Okay," she said. "Got to motor." Over her shoulder she said, "Love the dress, by the way. See ya!"

plainjain: omg, u will not believe who talked 2 me after school. who came up and talked to ME, on purpose. go on, guess.

malicious14: who?

plainjain: mary bryan richardson!!!

malicious14: wtf?

plainjain: and get this: she asked if i want 2 hang out sometime.

malicious14: haha, very funny

plainjain: she did, i swear. it was extremely freaky.

malicious14: did she have u confused w/somebody, u think?

malicious14: jk

plainjain: oh god, maybe she did. except she did use my name, so what's that all about?

malicious14: she probably felt sorry for u. she was probably like, "oh, there's that poor sad freshman who's always slinking off to the library."

plainjain: fyi, i didn't even go to the library. i was going to, but i changed my mind.

malicious14: why, cuz u were in a fog of post-mary bryan delirium? listen, jane, she might have SAID u should hang out, but she didn't really mean it. u know that, right?

plainjain: gee, thanks

malicious14: i'm just saying. anyway, i've g2g. i twisted my ankle during cheerleading practice, and i've gotta put more ice on it. everybody gave me those fake pity looks, when really they were just glad it wasn't them.

plainjain: bastards

plainjain: hey, maybe it was my dress, cuz mb did mention she liked it. u think that's it?

malicious14: mb? ur calling her mb now?

plainjain: i bet it was my dress.

malicious14: ur pathetic. bye!

I shut down the computer and shoved back my chair. It was on wheels, so it rolled back several feet before ramming into the coffee table.

"Jane," Mom warned from the kitchen.

"Sorry," I said.

We went through this at least once a day, all because Mom refused to let me put the computer in my room. She did it for my own good, so that I wouldn't become a raving sex maniac with the screen name "Foxxxie LaRue." This, from my thirty-nine-year-old thong-wearing mother.

She walked barefoot into the den. "All done with your homework?" she asked.

"Didn't have any," I said. "But I found this awesome site called 'jailbait.com.' Grown-ups visit it, not just kids, and I can sign up to be penpals with someone in prison. That would be okay, right? I could, like, give back to the community."

She sat on the worn sofa and patted the cushion beside her. "Come sit with me. Tell me about your day."

I rose from the computer chair and joined her.

"So what's new in Jane Land?" she asked.

"Nothing," I said. She scooched over her legs, and I leaned against her. "Alicia's trying out for cheerleading. She really, really, really wants to make it."

"Do you think she will?"

"Um, that would be a big fat no, sadly enough."

"Why not?"

"Because the more you want something, the less likely you are to get it. Anyway, she's kind of a spaz."

Mom stroked my hair. "Jane. You don't truly believe that, do you?"

"I'm not saying it to be mean. She's just not all that coordinated."

"No, that you never get the things you want."

I started to reply, then let my mind drift off as she traced circles on my scalp. It was like being little again, when she used to brush my hair after a bath. I'd smell like my special kid's shampoo that came in the fish-shaped bottle, and after the tangles had been combed out, Dad would wrap me in a hug and call me his mango-tango baby.

Mom kept caressing. After several minutes, she said, "Phil called, by the way. He didn't leave a message. He said it wasn't important."

"Okay," I said. Phil was my best boy bud. My safety date, not that I ever went on dates with him or anyone else. He'd kind of had a crush on me since we met in seventh grade—he tutored me in science for extra credit—but the good thing about Phil was that we could go on being friends and never really deal with it. I knew Phil would always be there for me.

"And your dad called," Mom continued. "He was sorry he missed you." Her fingers slowed in my hair. "He's flying to Zimbabwe tomorrow. He's going to stay in a thatched hut."

"Great," I said.

"Jane . . ."

"Mom."

She sighed. Now it was her turn not to reply.

I stared at the ceiling with its spiderweb of cracks. I listened to our breaths. Finally, I pushed myself up.

"Guess I better go to bed," I said.

Mom smiled up at me, although her eyes were sad. "Love you, Jane," she said.

"Yeah," I said. "Love you, too."

Upstairs, I pulled the teddy bear from my backpack. I stroked its fur, then lightly touched its nose.

It wasn't true, what Alicia had said about Dad. I didn't feel *abandoned*, boo-hoo-hoo. Because Dad hadn't abandoned us. That was giving him too much power. He'd just gone on a very long trip.

"Jane, your father needs some space to figure out who he is," Mom had said when Dad left three years ago. "He needs to do a lot of thinking. Nobody can do the work for him."

"But . . . what about us?" I'd asked.

"We'll be fine," Mom said. As in, case closed.

But another time I'd overheard her talking to her friend Kitty, who'd come over bearing beer and brownies. By that point half a year had gone by, and while Dad sent us checks to cover the bills, he still hadn't come home.

"Carol, you need help," Kitty had said. "Your gutters are in desperate need of cleaning, and the entire house could stand to be painted. Inside and out. Do you want me to send Dan over to take care of it?"

"No, thanks," Mom said. "I can handle it."

"Obviously you can't," Kitty said. "And you shouldn't have to. Honestly, Carol, this is getting ridiculous."

"You think I don't know that?" Mom replied. She was using her "marching bravely onward" voice, meant to keep pity at bay. "Yes, the house is falling apart. And yes, Carl should be here to take care of it—among other things, god knows. But I have to remind myself that things could be worse. At least he's not dead."

"Dead would be worse?"

Big silence. I could imagine the look Mom gave Kitty, because I'd received it often enough myself. But Kitty pressed on.

"Already you're without a husband, and poor Jane is without a father," she said. "Think what kind of damage that does to a kid."

From my spot on the stairs, I'd felt a welling of shame. Damaged goods, was that how Kitty saw me?

"Well, Kitty, life is messy," Mom said brusquely. "We don't always get to choose what happens to us, do we?"

"No, but we do get to choose how to respond."

I'd stood up, because I'd heard enough. Kitty was right: We did get to choose how to respond. And my response was to say screw it. Dad made his decisions, and I'd make mine, and nobody got to say I was damaged goods but me.

I still believed that, although believing it in my mind and believing it in my heart were sometimes two very different things. Because by staying away for so long, Dad didn't exactly make me feel as if I was worth sticking around for.

I turned the teddy bear upside down. It had soft felt pads on the bottoms of its paws, a detail I would have loved if I were still eleven. I opened my dresser drawer and dropped in the bear. I closed the drawer.

In the middle of the night, my eyes flew open. A dream, or a corner of one, had jerked me from sleep. Something about cheer-leading. Something about a boy. A boy in a raincoat.

Crap. It was Henry Huggins. Henry Huggins, from the Ramona books. He was Beezus's friend, the one with the paper route and the dog named Ribsy. And when Ramona was in kindergarten, he was the traffic boy that helped her cross the street. One stormy day she trudged into a muddy construction site and got stuck, and Henry lifted her straight out of her boots to safety.

The next day, Bitsy approached me at my locker. She wore a plaid micro-mini and a white Oxford with the sleeves rolled up. Her white knee socks were scrunched around her ankles, and on her feet she wore clunky Doc Martens. Her hair was tied back in doggy-ears.

"Hello, luv," she said.

My head jerked up, and I dropped my math spiral.

"Don't get your knickers in a twist," she said. "Can't a girl say hello?"

I bent to retrieve my notebook, cheeks burning. Chatting with Mary Bryan was one thing—and far weird enough to last for several days. But Bitsy? Bitsy was a junior, a full two years older than me. And she was British. She used expressions like "brilliant" and "pet" and "you stupid cow."

"Mary Bryan *did* talk to you, right?" Bitsy asked.

I nodded, focusing on her Hello Kitty hair elastics so I wouldn't have to meet her eyes. She was scarily hip.

"It's not a done deal, of course," she said. "We do have to test you."

"You do?" I felt like I was going to faint. I had no clue what she was talking about.

Bitsy tilted her head. "We're extremely selective, pet. We have to be. But we think you're the one."

The one *what*? I wanted to say. But I was too busy hyperventilating. Anyway, where was Alicia? We always met at our lockers first thing in the morning. If Alicia were here, she could tell me if this was really happening. And what it meant. Where *was* she?

"Wear something semi-nice," Bitsy said. "Not too tarty." She took in my T-shirt and jeans, which I'd worn over my everyday Jockeys for Her. I'd reverted to my pre–shopping spree basics, but I'd chosen my faded Sesame Street shirt with care, thinking it was maybe retro-cool.

"But maybe a little tarty wouldn't be bad, eh?" Bitsy laughed as she headed down the hall. "Friday night, then. Ta!"

Friday night, then? Friday night?! My only plans for Friday night were to curl up with a bag of popcorn and watch *Survivor: Senior High*. From last week's preview, I knew that the challenge involved a three-legged race to the school's infirmary while real gang members trolled the halls. There was supposed to be a twist, too. Something having to do with the team members' bandanas.

But Bitsy, was she suggesting . . . ?

I couldn't even say it in my head, that's how ridiculous it was. But if not that, then what? What *was* Bitsy suggesting?

I felt pressure behind my knees—a swift double nudge—and my legs buckled. I smelled Alicia's Obsession.

"Cute," I said, turning toward her.

"What did Bitsy want?" she asked. "I saw the two of you talking."

"Shit, Alicia, I have no idea. She just came up to me, out of the blue, and was all, 'Hello, luv,' and 'We think you're the one,' and—" I broke off. "What? Why are you staring at me like that?"

"The one what?" Alicia said.

"I have no idea! That's what I'm telling you! I mean, first Mary Bryan, and now Bitsy . . . it's just strange, that's all."

"I'll say," she said. Her expression wasn't happy. "I mean, last night when you mentioned Mary Bryan . . . but then I thought, 'No. No way.' Only now, if you're telling the truth . . ."

"What?!!" I said.

Alicia frowned. "Rae said they'd be picking a freshman. She said they always do."

Rae was Alicia's karaoke-singing sister, who'd graduated from Crestview five years ago. She still lived at home.

"'They' who?" I demanded. "And how would Rae know?"

"Because Rae went to school here before we did," Alicia said. Her tone said, *idiot.* "And there were Bitches back then, too."

I sighed. I knew what was coming was one of Rae's "back in the olden days" explanations, in which everything sucked because she was never homecoming queen or head cheerleader.

"Yeah, well, there've *always* been Bitches," I said. "And there will always be Bitches. It's just a fact of life."

"Exactly," Alicia said. "Only I didn't believe it at first."

"Believe what?"

She stared at me like I was a lab rat.

I turned to my locker and yanked out books. I knew it was going to be stupid, whatever Rae had told her, because it always was. Like not to let guys hug us from behind, because it was a sneaky way to cop a feel. Or not to put our hands in the front pockets of our jeans, because it might look like *we* were trying to cop a feel.

"Of *ourselves*?" I'd said when Rae laid that one on us.

"Keep your hands out of the cookie jar, that's all I'm saying," Rae had replied. She held up her own to show me, like *Hey, I've got nothing to hide.*

But stupid or not, I had to hear whatever Bitch-lore Rae had passed on.

"Fine," I said to Alicia. "Whatever it is, will you please just tell me?"

The bell rang for first period. Alicia glanced down the hall.

"I've got a Spanish quiz. I can't be late," she said.

"Alicia," I warned.

She turned back. She knew she had me. "Come over at five, after cheerleading practice. Rae can tell you herself."

🐈

I ate lunch in the library. Me and Ramona, age eight. This was the one in which Ramona accidentally broke an egg in her hair and got called a nuisance by her teacher, and as I turned the page, my heart went out to her. My heart did not go out to Alicia, and if she wondered why I wasn't in the cafeteria, it served her right. She could find someone else to eat with today. Like one of the feral cats, and she could go on and on to it about pikes and herkies and toe-touch jumps. I was just fine with Ramona, thanks very much.

A throat-clearing noise broke my concentration. I looked up, and there was Keisha. A senior. My heart started hammering.

"Hey," she said.

"Hey," I managed.

She gazed at me with her celery-colored eyes. Contacts, I was pretty sure, although some black people have green eyes. But I'd never seen anyone, black or white, with eyes that shade.

"Me and Mary Bryan and Bitsy, we hang together, right?" she said. "We're tight. Like sisters."

I nodded. My throat was dry.

"But we've got room for one more," she said. "A freshman."

I tried to keep my face blank, but my insides were knotting up because I had no idea what Keisha wanted from me. She wasn't smiling. In fact, she seemed pissed. But why would she be pissed at me? This was the first time I'd ever spoken to her.

She pressed her lips together. "So Friday you'll go to Kyle's party with us. We'll see how you fit in."

My stomach dropped. So did my book.

"Kyle . . . Kelley?" I asked.

She frowned, like *who else?*

But my mind refused to accept it. Kyle Kelley was a senior who threw legendary parties whenever his parents went out of town, and afterward there were stories of guys throwing up or girls doing lap dances or couples screwing around in Kyle's parents' bedroom and then passing out with half their clothes off.

Freshmen didn't go to Kyle's parties. Certainly not freshmen like me.

"Are you guys . . ." I started. "I mean, please don't take this the wrong way, but are you, like, playing a joke on me?"

I was amazed by my nerve. Pricks of sweat dinged under my arms.

"We don't play jokes," Keisha said. "It's not our style."

Ok-a-ay, I wanted to say. *But why me? Why, of all the fresh-man girls, would you possibly want me?* I wasn't in the popular crowd. I wasn't in the one-day-might-be-popular crowd. I was a dork who couldn't even pull off wearing a thong. I was Ramona, six years later, only instead of egg in my hair, I had—

Shit. I slapped my hand over the cover of my book, now splayed on the desk, which showed eight-year-old Ramona straddling her bike. Keisha inclined her head to see the title, and I slid Ramona to my lap.

"So," I said. "Uh . . ."

She straightened up. "Be ready at eight. We'll swing by and pick you up."

I gave her my widest smile. "Great. Fantastic."

"And don't be nervous. Just be yourself."

"Right. Um, thank you so much."

She looked at me funny, then strode from the carrel. My body went limp. They wanted me—maybe—to be one of them. They wanted me to be a Bitch.

"Rae!" Alicia called. She rapped hard on the bathroom door to be heard over the shower. "Jane's here. We want to talk to you."

"What?" Rae said.

"We need to talk to you!" Alicia said.

"I'm in the shower! I'm doing a mayonnaise rinse!"

Alicia scowled. "Come on," she said to me, marching down the hall. In her room, she flopped onto her bed, leaving me the option of the floor or the padded stool pushed under her vanity. I chose the floor.

"So . . . how was cheerleading practice?" I asked.

"Terrible," she said. "My voice cracked in the middle of 'Our Team Is Red Hot.'"

"Oh. Well, I bet no one noticed."

"Yeah, right. If you'd been there at lunch, you could have helped me practice—"

"In the cafeteria? With everyone watching?"

"—but noooo, you had to pull one of your stupid disappearing tricks because you were being a pouty-pants. I really could have used your support, you know. You're the only person who knows how important this is to me."

I was. It was true. Under Alicia's grouchy demeanor was a great ache of need, and I felt bad for letting her down.

"Anyway, one day you're going to be so busted," she said. "You're not supposed to have food in the library."

I sighed. A Nutrigrain bar here and there was not going to ruin civilization.

"Or maybe you were off being cool with MB," she accused. "Were you?"

"No," I said. "Although if you would hush for a minute, I'll tell you what did happen."

"Okay, tell me."

"Tell you what?" Rae asked, strolling into the room. She wore a T-shirt and panties, the front of which was damp from her pubic hair. I quickly raised my eyes to her face, which was just as startling, but in a different way. Rae was a permanent makeup artist, and as part of her training, she'd had permanent makeup applied to herself so she'd know what it felt like. And because she'd wanted it. So now, even though she'd just stepped out of the shower, her face looked perfectly made up.

Well, not *perfectly*. That was the startling part. The trainer who'd done the initial application had been too conservative for Rae's taste, so Rae had waited until she had her certificate and then she'd given herself a touch-up. Now her eyeliner was dark and thick, extending past her lids like catwoman. And she'd always thought her lips were too thin, so she'd gone back with the tattoo gun to make them look fuller. Now her lips were supersized. And very, very red.

"We're talking about the Bitches," Alicia said to Rae. "Tell Jane what you told me."

Rae turned and took me in. It was like being sized up by a damp mannequin. "You don't know?"

"Know *what*?" I said.

Rae walked across the floor and sat down with her back against Alicia's bed. She flipped her wet hair over her shoulders. "Well," she began, "they've been at Crestview for freaking ever. Not Keisha and Triscuit or whoever—"

"Bitsy," Alicia corrected. "And Mary Bryan Richardson."

"—but other girls. Other Bitches. One from each grade, four total. And always the most popular girls in school."

Inwardly, I groaned. She was acting as if this were privileged information, when anyone at school could have told me the same thing.

"When I was a freshman, the Bitch in my grade was Jennifer Mayfield," Rae said. "We all wanted to be her. We were so jealous we could spit. *Although . . .*" She paused dramatically. First she eyed Alicia, then she eyed me. "*We never did.* Spit, that is, or anything else that wouldn't be considered proper worshipping behavior. And you want to know why?"

I checked Alicia's reaction. Her legs were drawn to her chest, with her arms around her knees. Her black hair hung in bone-straight chunks. She jerked her chin, as if to say, *Ask, you fool. Aren't you even paying attention?*

"Why?" I said.

Rae tapped her thigh with violent purple nails. "Haven't you noticed that whenever they enter a room—your Bitches, my Bitches, whoever—everything stops and then starts up again, with them at the center of things?"

"Yeah," I said, like *so?*

"And haven't you noticed that even if you want to, you can't *not* like them?"

"Because no one would want to. Because they're . . ." I struggled for the right word, but couldn't find it. "Cool," I finished lamely.

"No," Rae said.

"Yes," I said.

"But that's not *why* you like them."

"Yes it is."

"No it's not."

"Yes it *is.*"

"*No,* it's *not.*"

I closed my eyes. Conversations with Rae were always like this. They went on and on and when they finally ended, the payoff was zilch. *Don't jam your hands in your front pockets, or else.*

I opened my eyes. I raised my eyebrows at Alicia, who raised hers right back.

"Fine," I said to Rae. "Then why *do* I like them, if it's not because they're cool?"

"Because you have to. Because they *make* you."

"And how do they do that?"

"I don't know. But they do."

"Uh-huh. Mind control? Voodoo? Invisible puppet strings?"

Rae regarded me with disdain. "Crack jokes if it makes you feel better. But the world is a hell of a lot bigger than you think. All sorts of things go on that you know nothing about."

Alicia scooted closer. "Finish telling her about Jennifer Mayfield."

"Oh yeah," I said. "Definitely."

"Well, like I said, Jennifer was tapped to be a Bitch," Rae said. She got to her knees and stretched her body, reaching for the brush on Alicia's dresser. She grasped it and sat back down. "But it fell apart."

"What do you mean, it fell apart?"

Rae tugged at the tangles in her hair. "She pissed them off. Or else she just wasn't good enough. She never figured it out."

"Did she care?"

"Did she *care*? She *only* switched schools in the middle of fall semester. She *only* ran away with her tail between her legs and never came back. Uh, yeah, I'd say she cared."

Okay, I could get that. I was starting to care, too. "So what does that have to do with Bitsy and Mary Bryan and Keisha?"

"Everything," Rae said. "Because Jennifer let things slip before she left. And the Bitches aren't all they appear to be. That's all I'm saying."

"But Bitsy and Keisha and Mary Bryan weren't around when you and Jennifer were in high school. They'd have been in, like, elementary school."

"Have you been listening to anything I've said? They're all the same, year after year after year. They may not start out that way, but then they *do* something. Something big. And they *become*."

"Become?" I repeated.

"I don't know how, no one does, but there's more going on than everyone thinks." Rae stopped brushing. She lowered her voice. "Something bad happened a long time ago. Really bad."

"And that would be?"

She tilted her head. "Have you ever heard the saying, 'She sold her soul to the devil'?"

Oh good god. "Rae," I said, "I'm not a little kid straight out of the pumpkin patch. I stopped being scared of ghost stories years ago."

Rae's expression didn't change. Her face was long, and there was nothing in her manner that suggested she was kidding. Despite myself I got a chill.

"The school covered it up, but everyone knows," she said.

"Not me," I said.

Rae gazed at me. "There was a girl. Her name was Sandy. She cared too much what people thought of her, because she was super needy. She really, really, really wanted to be popular."

Yeah, well, who doesn't? I thought. Although the term "needy" made me shift uncomfortably.

"She joined with three others," Rae went on. "One from each grade."

"They were losers, too," Alicia put in. "Right, Rae?"

Rae plowed on. "But Sandy was the one who did it."

"Did what?" I asked. I plucked at my jeans, then made myself stop. I told my body to relax.

"They went to an empty storage room in Hamilton Hall," Rae said. "One of those rooms where no one ever goes—"

"Up on the third floor," Alicia contributed.

"—and performed a ritual in the dead of night." Rae leaned forward. "They offered a sacrifice, and the sacrifice was accepted."

"What . . . was it?" I said. I couldn't believe I was asking.

"They awakened some weird creepy power—and I'm not making this up," Rae said. "That shit is out there, like when you feel someone watching you, only when you turn around there's no one there. Or like when you do the Ouija board, and it really does work."

"That happened at Lisette's slumber party, in seventh grade," Alicia said. "You remember, Jane. It said that a boy whose name started with a C was going to ask Lisette out, and one week later she was going steady with Casper Langdon."

Rae silenced Alicia with a look of disdain. To me, she said, "I'm telling you, it's out there. Shit that no one sees."

My heart was doing something I didn't like. I swallowed and repeated my question. "What did they sacrifice?"

Rae pressed her oversized lips in a line. "A cat."

"A *cat*?" My tension broke, and a laugh, or something like it, squeezed out of me. For a second there . . . all that bullshit about deserted schools and the dead of night . . . but Rae's whole story was ridiculous. Next she'd be telling me that's why the feral cats had taken over the school. As payback, or because they were spooks, or because they now had to haunt the place where the first had been slain. Demon cats. Devil cats. *Ooooo-oooo.*

Rae got angry. "They slit its throat. Or rather, Sandy did. You think that's funny?"

"Yes," I said.

"And then she died."

"Well, duh, that's what happens when your throat gets slit." I felt buoyant. My lungs had lost their tightness.

"Not the cat," Rae said sharply. "Sandy."

Nuh-uh, she wasn't getting me again. "Oh, please."

"And her soul . . . it fed the power. Made it grow stronger."

"You are so full of it," I said.

"And *that's* what created the Bitches." Rae got to her feet. "That's why you like them, because you have no choice."

"Why wasn't it in the papers?" I asked. "Why wasn't the school shut down?"

She looked at me in a way that was supposed to make me think she felt sorry for me. She huffed out of the room, taking Alicia's brush with her.

"It's not funny, Jane," Alicia said angrily. "It's, like, witchcraft. *Real* witchcraft."

"Only it's not *witch*craft, it's *Bitch*craft," I said. I giggled at my wit, but Alicia didn't crack a smile.

"You need to stay clear of them," she said.

I leaned back on my elbows and crossed one foot over the other. I let my head drop back so that the ends of my hair grazed the carpet. "Thanks, Alicia. I'll take it under advisement."

Later that night, I phoned Phil.

"Janie!" he said, his voice all happy. "Hey!"

"Mom said you called last night. Sorry I didn't call back." Which was true, in a general sort of way, but I wasn't worried because I knew Phil wouldn't hold a grudge. "So what's up?"

"Not much," he said. "Just wanted to tell you how hot you looked in that blue dress you wore."

"Ha, ha," I said. This was the kind of thing Phil did, throw out a compliment in a joking way so that it didn't have to mean anything. Because "hot" was such a stud-boy word, and Phil was so not a stud.

"I mean it," he said. "I wanted to tell you at school, only I didn't want the other guys to notice and start slobbering all over you."

"Uh-huh," I said. These days Phil and I were more out-of-school friends, anyway. Partly because our classes didn't overlap, but also because when we were in school, Phil had other stuff to worry about, like guys dumping his lunch and giving him flats. Phil was kind of scrawny, and he liked science more than sports, which made him an obvious target. Plus, he'd never developed that cynical veneer that Crestview guys thought was all important. Phil was an eager beaver in a school that didn't give a damn.

I sat on my bed and kicked off my shoes. I lay back and stared at the ceiling, at the frosted-glass light fixture that had been there since the dawn of time. Dead bugs made dark splotches in its center. "So want to hear something weird?"

"Sure."

"I'm going to a party Friday night. *With the Bitches.* Isn't that insane?"

"Whoa," Phil said. "Hold on there, filly."

"I know. It's crazy. Unless it's a joke—do you think it's a joke?"

Because that was the angle Alicia had taken, after I failed to be suitably cowed by the Bitchcraft theory. I'd told her about Kyle's party, and she'd shifted tactics, saying, "But what if it's one of those 'ugly' parties, where whoever brings the ugliest date wins?" She bit at a cuticle. "You're not seriously going to go, are you?"

Phil's voice pulled me back. "I hope you're planning on filling me in, because I have zero clue what you're talking about."

"Right. Sorry." I rolled onto my side, switching the phone to my unsquished ear. I told him everything except for Rae's mumbo-jumbo, then said, "But why would they pick me? That's the part that makes no sense. Unless I'm their ugly date. Am I? Am I their ugly date?"

"Geez, Janie, are you blind?" Phil said. "You're so beautiful, you make my teeth ache."

"Be serious. I'm, like, socially retarded. Especially compared to Keisha and Bitsy and Mary Bryan."

He fell silent. He was probably getting a hard-on thinking about them, which was surprisingly depressing. Even though I knew Phil was a boy, and all boys liked the Bitches, I was used to him liking only me.

"Keisha and Bitsy are way beyond hot," he finally said, "and I'd be lying if I said I'd throw them out of my bed. And Mary Bryan's an absolute sweetheart. She's got French at the same time as I have geometry, and our rooms are right across from each other. Sometimes I catch myself just . . . watching for her, you know?"

I nodded. For some dumb reason I was afraid I was going to cry.

"But none of them holds a candle to you, Janie. Want to know why?"

"Why?"

"Because you're a good person," he said. "Because you try to do the right thing."

"I do? Like when?"

"Come on, don't be so hard on yourself."

I wanted to ask again, because I really wanted to know. But even with Phil, I couldn't be that pathetic.

"I should go," I said. "I should make myself go to bed."

"Yeah, me too. See you tomorrow?"

"Uh-huh. I'll be the one rescuing kitty cats and saving the world."

"Super Janie," he said. "You could wear a T-shirt with a big red J."

"A leotard, like Wonder Woman. With huge red undies."

He laughed, and I pressed the off button on my phone.

In bed, as shadows played on my walls, my thoughts spiraled back to Rae's story about four girls who would do anything to be popular. Silly, stupid story—yet in the dark, even stupid stories misbehaved.

I remembered something Mom told me once, about two girls in her hometown. They'd snuck to a cemetery late at night, because they'd heard that if you stuck a knife into a fresh-laid grave, its ghost would rise from the dead. One of the girls knelt on the grave and plunged the knife deep. She tried to stand up, but she couldn't, and she screamed that the ghost had grabbed her. The other girl fled, and when she returned with her parents, she found her friend collapsed over the grave, no longer breathing. She'd stabbed her nightgown when she'd stabbed the grave, pinning herself to the ground. Her panic overcame her, which meant she'd basically died of fright.

Although, come on. As I replayed the story in my head, I realized that it couldn't have really happened. What teenager has ever died of fright? It was just a story Mom passed on after hearing it from a friend, from someone whose brother's cousin's fiancé had actually known the two girls. Or whatever. It was a story Mom told me for fun, to make goose bumps prick my arms.

But stories couldn't hurt you.

I imagined four girls giggling as they made their way to Crestview's empty storage room, the beams of their flashlights skittering off the walls.

And then, at some point, the giggling would have stopped.

I dreamed of cats, of sharp claws tapping through darkened halls.

Wednesday was a waste. Thursday was a bigger waste. In the daylight hours Rae's story faded to just a whisper, but the fact of the Bitches remained, making me hyperaware of everything I did. How I held myself, how I talked, how I laughed. And all because of the remote possibility that one of the Bitches might be around to notice.

"Could you give it a rest?" Alicia said during study hall. She'd been leaning forward, obsessing out loud about her latest cheerleading drama, but now she flung herself back in her chair. "They're not here, Jane."

"Who's not here?" I asked. When she didn't buy it, I said, "I was listening. I was. You said that for the tryout, you have to be able to do a split or you're eliminated."

"I said you *don't* have to do a split. You can just squat if you have to, which you would have known if you weren't so busy acting dramatic." She widened her eyes and gave a fake gasp. She drew her hand to her chest. *"A split?"* she mimicked. *"You have to do a split?!"*

I felt myself blush. I glanced around, praying the Bitches really weren't here.

"God," Alicia said. "You're embarrassing yourself and you don't even know it."

I twisted the metal wire of my spiral notebook, because I *did* know it. Other people acted natural in group situations, no problem. But not me. Especially when there was a chance someone might see.

Alicia gathered her books and shoved them into her backpack. "Stupid me, I thought you actually cared about my boring, pathetic life."

"I do," I protested.

"Uh-huh." She glared. "Well, all I can say is that if you do become popular, you have to take me with you. Swear?"

I groaned. "I thought you said to stay clear of them. I thought you said they were evil." I made spooky fingers, which she swatted away.

"I did, and they are," she said. "Do you swear?"

This was so like Alicia, to warn me away from something— saying it was for my own good—and then want that very thing if there was a chance it might really come through. Would I take Alicia, if given the opportunity? Would she take me if the situation were reversed? It sounded so stupid, *you have to take me with you.* As if it were a prison break.

"Oh my god," Alicia said, and I realized I'd taken too long with my answer.

"I swear, I swear," I said.

"I'm leaving. You've given me a headache."

"Sorry," I said.

"Yeah?" she said. "You should be."

Didn't see the Bitches in the hall. Didn't see the Bitches in the bathroom. Didn't see the Bitches in the library, where I ate lunch in order to avoid pissy Alicia.

I did, however, see Camilla Jones. Camilla was a freshman, like me and Alicia, although she often forgot to act like it. She read battered textbooks on post-modernism, for example, and she used words like "socio-economic" even when teachers weren't around. Today she wore a dusty rose leotard and a wrap-around skirt, and she'd secured her bun with serviceable brown bobby pins. She always wore her hair in a bun, because she was really serious about ballet. Ballet and weird literature theory shit, those were Camilla's things.

Looking at Camilla, what occurred to me was, *Huh. She's not obsessed with the Bitches.* This was a new thought, and I tested it in my mind to see if it held up. At lunch, Camilla usually sat with the drama kids, although she invariably kept her nose buried in one of her books. Did she get all twittery when the Bitches entered the cafeteria? I didn't think so. I didn't think Camilla got twittery, period. And I couldn't remember her ever complimenting one of the Bitches or getting tongue-tied around them or gazing at them surreptitiously from across the room.

No. I was sure she didn't. Which meant that Rae was a big juicy freak, as of course I'd known all along.

I crumpled my granola bar wrapper and stood up. I walked over to Camilla's carrel.

"Hey," I said. I didn't really know why.

She lifted her head. She seemed surprised that anyone was talking to her.

"Um . . . what are you reading?" I asked.

She flipped her book so I could see. It was called *Artifacts of Popular Culture.*

"Huh. Is it any good?"

"It's all right," she said. She paused, then added, "Did you know that Barbie dolls can grasp wine glasses, but not pens?"

"Pens? You mean, like to write with?"

"And Astronaut Barbie's spacesuit is pink, with puffed sleeves."

Her disgust was apparent, so instead of saying, "Well, that's to make her look cute," I kind of laughed and said, "Yeah, that's definitely what I'd wear if I were an astronaut. Well . . . see you!"

I left, and my brain spun back to the Bitches. Maybe Camilla was impervious to their charms, but I wasn't, especially after they'd lavished me with one-on-one attention. Why had they treated me that way only to leave me in the cold?

See? I told myself. *It was a joke. They were stringing you along for their own amusement, and now they're done. What were you thinking—that your life was honestly going to change?*

Then I came back with, *But who said anything about hanging out together at school? Not Keisha. Not Bitsy. Not Mary Bryan. Maybe the hanging-out part comes later, after you pass the test.*

And then my stomach got spazzy and I had a panic attack right there in the hall. Kyle's party was only a day away, and what if the Bitches didn't arrive to pick me up? What if they *did*?

During my humanities elective on early religions, as Lurl the Pearl tried to explain parthenogenesis to Bob Foskin for the hundredth time, I claimed a vacant research computer and spread out my notes so that it would look like I was working on the day's assignment. The Camilla factor had punched a hole in Rae's "powers from beyond" theory, but I thought I'd Google the Bitches and see what came up. Even though I knew it would be nothing.

"Nossir," Bob Foskin complained from his desk at the front of the room. "Just ain't no way a chick can make a baby on her own, goddess or no goddess."

"Fertility. Creation. Rebirth," Lurl the Pearl droned in her gravelly voice. "There are mysteries in the world that aren't meant to be understood."

"I don't know nothing about that," Bob said. "What I do know is that every mare needs a stallion, if you catch my drift."

A few kids tittered, but I tuned them out. I jiggled the computer's mouse, and the "Lady and the Beast" screen saver disappeared. When I got to Google, I typed in "Sandy," "Crestview Academy," and after a moment of thought, "died." No hits, of course. I tried "Crestview" and "witchcraft," but again got no hits. I cleared the search line and typed in "bitches," just for the hell of it. The list I got filled zillions of pages. First came the obligatory "female dog" stuff, and then the entries got more interesting. Tokyo Bitches, IQ Bitches, Cricket-playing Bitches. I found one site called Mature Bitches, which must have slipped past the school's blocking software, because when I pulled it up, I was bombarded with porn pop-ups. If I ever needed a perverted granny, I knew where to go.

Something brushed my leg, and I jumped. A cat—small and dark with clumpy fur. The feral cats were always prowling around in here, probably because Lurl the Pearl was the sole teacher who didn't seem to mind. And usually I didn't either. Usually I felt sorry for them, because they were so mangy and bedraggled. Other students complained—a girl named Alice was allergic and brought in a note from her doctor—but Lurl the Pearl didn't do anything about it. "Focus, please," she'd said, blankly surveying both the class and the cats.

The cat nudged me again and let out a squeaky mew. *Usually* I didn't mind—but today I didn't want to touch it. Rae's story had done that if nothing else. But I didn't want to not touch it, either, just because of Rae's malarkey. I gave the cat a quick scratch, then wiped my hand on my jeans and scrolled further down the list on my computer. Chess Bitches, Vegan Bitches, Snarky Bitches . . . hmm. The description for Snarky Bitches read, "For girls/women who are Bitches, plain and simple." I double clicked on the address. The screen blipped, and a hot pink site logo popped up.

"Have we finished the assignment?" Lurl the Pearl asked from behind me.

I smothered a cry. She was mouth breathing down my neck. Quickly I clicked the back button, and the list of "bitch" sites reappeared. *Shit, shit, shit.* I clicked again and again to get back to the Google homepage.

"This computer is reserved for research, Miss Goodwin," said Lurl the Pearl. "Not Internet hanky panky."

"Sorry, Ms. Lear," I said. I swiveled to face her, reminding myself not to stare at the bizarre contraption connected to her rose-tinted glasses. But it was extremely difficult. A thick strip of elastic circled her head like a crown, securing a Band-Aid shaped piece of metal that stretched horizontally across her pale fore-head. A slimmer piece of metal extended downward from the Band-Aid's center and hooked the bridge of her glasses, prevent-ing them from slipping out of place. All of this to save her the effort of pushing them up every now and then.

She blinked. "In any case, we do not condone the exploration of inappropriate subjects. Let's save the nasty until we're safe at home, shall we?"

The nasty?

"I wasn't . . . I mean, I was just . . ." My gaze strayed to the metal T. I wondered if she got tan lines from it, or if it got hot and burned her. I wondered if she ever went out in the sun.

The cat at my feet mewed, and Lurl scooped it up. It immediately began to purr.

"In any case, you won't find what you were looking for on the computer," she said. She did this laugh thing that sounded like a grown man's giggle, and my internal creep-meter dinged in alarm.

"Um, I really don't know what you're talking about. I swear."

She stopped giggling. "Focus, please," she said, fondling the cat as it head-butted her hand. She turned to face the class. "Would anyone care to discuss the cult objects found in the temple of Kali, goddess of death and resurrection?"

Friday night, Bitsy pulled up in front of my house at eight-fifteen.

"My, aren't we looking glam?" she said when she saw me. "Quite a bit of leg on show there, eh?" She and Mary Bryan went into a titter fest, and my insides gummed up. I couldn't move.

"Hi, Jane," Keisha said from the passenger seat of Bitsy's red car. "Get in."

I searched Keisha's face. She didn't *seem* to be joking.

"Come on, come on," Bitsy said. "You're dead lucky I haven't peeled off by now."

I climbed past Keisha into the back. I squished in with Mary Bryan and tugged at my skirt.

"Don't let Bitsy bother you," Mary Bryan said. "Anyway, I love your blouse."

"Really? It's not too see-through?"

Mary Bryan tucked my bra strap under the strap of the camisole. "There. Fabulous."

"*You* look fabulous," I told her. I leaned forward to address Bitsy and Keisha. "You guys, too. You look great."

"Thanks, Jane," Keisha said. "You're sweet."

Bitsy accelerated, and I fell back against my seat. Mary Bryan giggled.

"So help us out, will you, luv?" Bitsy said over her shoulder. "I want the truth. Your honest opinion."

"On what?"

"Nose rings. Not a hoop, just a stud. A tiny silver star, for example."

"Oh my god," Mary Bryan moaned. "Bitsy!"

I pushed myself into a more comfortable position. "Uh . . . in general, or on someone specific?"

"On me," Mary Bryan said. "She's talking about me, because I happened to mention—*once*!—that I thought it might look cute. But I wasn't going to actually *do* it."

"Right, now you deny it," Bitsy said. "So what about it, Jane? Yay or nay?"

Mary Bryan hid her face in her hands. "Go on. Just say it, whatever it is."

I hesitated. I could tell they were teasing, but I wasn't sure how to proceed. "Well, I wouldn't judge somebody for getting it done," I hedged. "Because, I mean, it's their body. They can do whatever they want."

"Ha," Mary Bryan said. "See?"

"But would *you* get it done?" Bitsy said. "Would you even consider it?"

"Personally? Um, probably not?"

"*Exactly*," Bitsy said. She caught my eye in the rearview mirror. "Good girl, Jane."

"Sorry," I said to Mary Bryan.

"I never said I was actually going to do it," she said.

Keisha turned toward the window, but she was smiling. My chest filled with something balloony and light.

Bitsy tapped her iPod to change the playlist. She punched up the volume and tapped the beat on the steering wheel.

Feeling bold, I fingered the hem of my skirt. "So, what you said about showing a lot of leg. Is that a good thing? Or do I look, you know, too tarty?"

I meant it to be flippant. An I-can-take-it sort of remark, and also to show that I hadn't forgotten what she'd said that day by my locker. But she and Keisha exchanged a look, and my stomach dipped.

"What?" I said.

Keisha twisted in her seat to face me. "Listen, Jane. Don't take this the wrong way, but looks *do* matter. And if you're going to be one of us, you've got to meet a certain standard. Do you know what I'm saying?"

Mary Bryan found my hand and squeezed it.

Keisha pressed on. "Your skirt's a little short. I'm not going to lie. But for the most part you're cute enough. And you do all right in school, which isn't that important, but it doesn't hurt. All of this is part of why we chose you. But you know what the most important thing is?"

I shook my head.

"You have to *want* it," Keisha said. "You have to want to be popular more than you've wanted anything in your life."

Her eyes bored into me. Was I supposed to say something? Was I supposed to, like, bounce up and down and do cheerleader jumps?

Without meaning to, I thought of the dead girl, Sandy, who had somehow come to life in my brain even though I knew she had never existed. Sandy, who was super needy. Who really, really, really wanted to be popular.

"And we know you do," Mary Bryan said reassuringly. "Right, Jane?"

"Crikey, here we are," Bitsy said. She turned left into a gated community and pulled up at the guard station. She gave them Kyle's name.

"So . . . what do I need to do?" I asked. I heard my voice quaver, and I dug my fingernails into my palms.

Keisha's expression softened. "Your wardrobe needs some work—it's true. But you're here at Kyle's party with us. You're pulling up in Bitsy's car, and you're walking in the door with Mary Bryan on one side of you and me on the other. Okay?"

The gate creaked open.

"Just be cool, luv," Bitsy said. "Tonight you're our baby Bitch."

I tried. I *did*. But my gut cramped up the second I walked in the door, and the whole time I was there I felt like I needed to sprint to the bathroom. Plus, everything was all chichi and ultra fancy. Like, there was a plaque in the entry hall announcing that this was a SHOE-FREE ENVIRONMENT. A shoe-free environment? In all my fourteen years, not once had I seen a plaque announcing a shoe-free environment.

The others slipped off their shoes and put them on a special rack, so I stepped out of my clogs and did the same thing. My toenails were scraggly. I tried to scrunch them out of view.

"Ladies," Kyle said, swooping over to greet us. He put one arm around Bitsy and one arm around Mary Bryan. "Bitsy, I adore that halter. And Keisha! Our queen of the Nile!" He let go of Bitsy and Mary Bryan and air-kissed Keisha's cheek.

"Hi, Kyle," Keisha said. She returned his kiss and made eyes at Bitsy.

Kyle stepped back. He gave me the once over. "Well, what do we have here?"

My face split into a twitchy grin. "Hi," I said. "Thanks for inviting me to your party."

"You're very welcome. *Did* I invite you to my party?"

My smile hurt the sides of my mouth.

"Kyle, this is Jane," Bitsy said. "Be nice."

"Oh, poo. I'm always nice." He looped his arm through mine and led me toward the kitchen. "Jane. *Jane.* Can I offer you a quencher, Jane?"

"Uh, sure," I said. "Thanks."

"Don't thank me yet, cupcake. What'll you have?"

I looked at the blue- and gold-tiled countertops, which were lined with bottles. Dewar's. Grey Goose. Bacardi. I remembered a drink I'd heard mentioned in a movie. "Maybe a mojito?"

"Aren't we sophisticated," Kyle said.

Bitsy choke-laughed. But she said, "Make it two. Better yet, four. I think we could all benefit from a mojito, right, girls?"

She lounged against the counter, as comfortable in her body as I was uncomfortable in mine. I modeled my position after hers. *Chill*, I told myself. *You are here with the Bitches. You are golden.*

Kyle handed me my drink. It tasted like mint.

From where I stood I could see the already crowded living room, and out of everyone there—the jocks and the cheerleaders, the honor council kids, the partiers—there wasn't a single person I knew well enough to say hello to. So when Keisha said, "All right, Jane. Time to mingle," I about crapped my pants.

"I'll just hang out here," I said. "But, you know, thanks."

"We need to see you in action," Keisha said.

Panicked, I turned to Mary Bryan.

"You can do it," she said. She smiled anxiously. "It'll be fun."

Bitsy raised her glass. "Go on, luv. Strut your stuff."

Elizabeth Greene, head cheerleader: . . . and so he called me up out of the blue and was like, "I could really use someone to cuddle with right now." Isn't that too cute?

Amy Skyler, Elizabeth's best friend: No.

Elizabeth: I think he wants to get back together.

Amy: Elizabeth, he was *horny.* Which, in case you've forgotten, is why he dumped you for Paisley in the first place.

Elizabeth: She totally stole him on purpose. Slut.

Amy: Skank.

Elizabeth: Lying piece of trash.

Me, edging closer: Paisley Karr? The girl who trains Seeing-Eye dogs?

Elizabeth: Who the fuck are you?

Stuart Hill, star quarterback: Dude! I am all about faith. I mean, those Christian girls are hot.

John Rogers, linebacker: Yeah, man. You said it.

Me:

Stuart: I'm like, "You want to pray, sweet thing? Sure, baby, get
   down on those knees."

John, cackling: Forgive me, O Lord, for I have sinned.

Me:

Stuart: *Dude!*

🐈

Raven Holtzclaw-Fontaine, super-good artist: I'm dying to
   capture one of them in oil. Those claws. Those yellow eyes.
   Oh my god, those *tails.*

Katie Clark, wannabe artist: You should. You totally should.

Raven: "Doomed to Die," I could call it. Or, I know, I know. "Fish
   out of Water."

Katie, giggling: "Fish" out of water? Not "cat" out of water?

Raven: It's a statement, Katie, not a one-to-one
   correspondence.

Me: Are you, um, talking about the feral cats?

Katie: Excuse me?

Me: Because even though they're creepy, I kind of feel bad for
   them. Don't you? I mean, they just want to go about their
   lives, but they can't, because everybody hates them and
   throws rocks at them and—

Raven, coldly: Well, that's their own fault. Did anyone force
   them to make their little love nests on our fucking
   campus? No.

Me: Oh. That's true, I guess, only—

Katie: Ex*cuse* me, but I don't think we asked for your
   opinion. So if you don't mind . . . ?

By ten, I was ready to throw myself over a cliff. Here I was supposed to be strutting my stuff, and my stuff was utterly pathetic.
Hell, had the Bitches wanted to show how unfit I was for the
whole popularity game, they couldn't have picked a better way.

I even made a fool of myself in front of Nate Solomon, a senior
I'd had a secret crush on since before the school year started. Nate
lived next door to Phil, and all summer long I'd gotten to admire him
from Phil's backyard. Polishing the hood of his pickup. Buffing the
fenders with his T-shirt, which he'd have conveniently taken off. His
arms were such boy arms, strong and muscular. Sometimes I got so
mesmerized that I lost track of Phil altogether.

"Janie," Phil would say. "*Janie.* Anyone there?"

"Ooo, sorry," I'd say, "I just got distracted." I'd flash Phil my
most charming smile. "What was that again?"

So when I spotted Nate shuffling through CDs by Kyle's
stereo, my heart whomped so hard I thought I would be sick. *This
is your chance,* I coached myself. *This is your only, only chance.* I
swallowed and made myself step forward.

"Um, hi," I said.

His eyes flicked over me. He grunted.

"So . . . picking out some music?" I blushed the second I said it, because duh, what else did I think he was doing? Strumming a banjo? But it didn't matter, because his attention had already slid elsewhere.

"Ryan!" he called, holding one CD aloft. "Ice bonus, man!"

He brushed past me on the way to the CD player and didn't notice as he knocked my shoulder, because I was absolutely invisible.

Humiliated, I slunk to the kitchen. The tile counters and the top of the island were cluttered with plastic cups and half-full wineglasses, but there were no actual people in the room. It was a party-free zone, at least for the moment. I bit my lip, then crossed to the far side of the island. I slid down behind it, bringing my knees to my chest as my butt reached the floor. I was eye level with the cabinets under the sink. A lone blue M&M rested on the floor by a piece of fluff.

I exhaled. All that was left of my mojito were small ovals of ice, and I sucked a piece into my mouth. I let it drift about my tongue, then leaned slightly forward and let it slip out. I swirled my glass until I couldn't distinguish it from the others.

In the living room, someone shrieked and said, "Turn that thing off! I look terrible!"

"Ah, shut up. You know you love it," a guy said. Stuart Hill, who was apparently making the rounds with his video camera again. I'd seen him with it earlier in the night.

The tension in my chest started to loosen—the party people were *there*, and I was *here*—and I had the thought that I could stay hidden behind the island forever. It was clean. It was dry. It was actually quite comfortable. I raised my glass and slurped in another ice oval, then choked as I heard feet pad across the tiled kitchen floor.

"—in common at all," a girl was saying. "I'm just so tired of it."

I swallowed the ice and drew my knees up as far as I could.

There was the hiss of an opened pop top. A second girl said, "Tell me about it. All I think about is what a good girlfriend I would be, if only I got the chance."

I breathed as quietly as I could. The first girl was Sukie Karing, I was pretty sure. And the second girl was Pammy Varlotta, another junior. I could tell by the way she pronounced her Ts, as if her tongue was too big for her mouth.

"I mean, seriously," Pammy went on. "How sad is that?"

A third girl laughed. Even before she spoke, I knew who it was.

"Dead sad," Bitsy said. "If you want a boy, Pammy, you've got to go out and get yourself one. None of this lurking about feeling sorry for yourself."

Shit, shit, shit. Sweat beaded the nape of my neck.

"Easy for you to say," Sukie said. "You've got boys drooling over you every time you turn around."

"Well . . ." Bitsy said.

"But she's with Brad now," Pammy interjected. "Right, Bitsy? And I'm *so* happy for you. You're such a great couple."

"Yeah? You don't think he's a bit flash?" Bitsy asked.

"Oh my god, he's the hottest guy in school," Pammy said. "Not to mention the fact that he totally worships you."

Even in my nervousness, I gagged at what a suck-up Pammy was. On the other hand, if I were in her place, I'd probably be licking Bitsy's boots, too. If Bitsy were wearing boots. If it were a shoe-possible environment.

"There is that," Bitsy said. A chip bag rustled. "I suppose I'll keep him a little longer."

"Good, because we don't want you single again, that's for sure," Pammy said. She giggled. "Little Miss Greedy-Guts, stealing all the boys away."

There was a pause. Then, "Little Miss Greedy-Guts?"

"She didn't mean it like that," Sukie interjected. "Right, Pammy? She just meant—"

"What if I want to be Little Miss Greedy-Guts?" Bitsy asked, dangerously smooth.

Pammy's giggles dried up. "I just . . . it's just that you're so beautiful and funny, and your accent is so adorable. None of us has a chance when you're around."

"Maybe none of you has a chance because you're whining slags," Bitsy said.

Sukie tried to laugh. "Bitsy. Don't be like that."

"Like what? Honest?"

A drip of condensation rolled down my glass.

"Every boy in the school wants to go out with you, that's all," Sukie said. "I mean, not that it's your fault."

"Of course not!" Pammy chimed in. "I never meant it was your *fault.* Oh my god, is that what you thought?"

"It's just a fact of life," Sukie went on. "You think Payton would be going out with me if he thought he had a shot with you?"

"And Ryan Overturf," Pammy said. "Last year he wouldn't give me a second look. He was all Bitsy, Bitsy, Bitsy. But now that you're with Brad—"

"Enough," Bitsy commanded.

They both shut up. I gripped my glass.

But when Bitsy spoke again, it was in a new voice. "So, Pammy. You fancy Ryan, do you?"

"I don't know," Pammy said hesitantly. "Maybe? And I think— I mean, probably not—but sometimes I think maybe he likes me back?"

"Oh, he likes you. No worries there, luv."

Now Bitsy was being *too* nice. It worried me.

"Really?" Pammy said. Her hopefulness was excruciating "Has he . . . has he said something to you?"

Bitsy laughed. "Not just to me. To anyone who'll listen."

"Bitsy . . ." Sukie said.

Pammy started hyperventilating. "Oh my god, oh my god. You have to tell me!"

"Well, you do know he drives by your house practically every night, right?" Bitsy said. "Sometimes he parks at the corner and just moons up at the house."

"He does?"

"He says you leave your curtains open, you sly dog. He says it's quite the peep show."

"He says—what?"

"Says you've got quite good form, really. The whole innocent school girl act, prancing before the mirror in matching bra and panties . . ."

Pammy's confusion made her stupid. "*What?* I don't . . . I swear, I never—"

"Look, pet, I think it's brilliant," Bitsy soothed. "Give him a taste and make him beg for more. Him and all the other blokes he's told."

"He's lying," Pammy whispered. "I don't leave my curtains open, I swear."

Feet slapped the floor. "Ladies, ladies," a male voice said. *Kyle.* "Your presence is required. We're starting a game of butt quarters."

"Butt quarters, ooo goody," Bitsy said. "Sukie, Pammy? You in?"

Pammy sniffled. "I . . . I need to go to the bathroom," she said. She fled the room.

"Good grief," Kyle said, clearly confused. "Was she *crying?*"

"Here, Kyle," Bitsy said. "Have some chips." The bag rattled. Kyle crunched.

"Did Ryan really say all that?" Sukie asked in an undertone.

"She really should be more careful," Bitsy replied.

"For Christ's sake, these chips are stale," Kyle complained. "That is the last time I buy organic, the environment be damned."

"Abso-bloody-lutely," Bitsy said. "Preservatives or die."

Kyle strode past the island to the pantry, and my blood froze. He stood within feet of my hiding spot. "There must be a bag of Tostitos stashed around here somewhere."

My heart whammed. I trained my gaze on the floor—not on his khakis, not on his pale feet—and prayed he would find the chips and leave. *Please, please, please,* I prayed.

"Ta-da," he called.

I screwed my eyes shut.

He headed for the living room. "Shall we, then? Butt quarters awaits."

"I better check on Pammy," Sukie said.

"Suit yourself," said Bitsy. "Kyle—hold up!"

The kitchen emptied, except for me. I crawled out from behind the island. Leftover adrenaline pumped through my veins. I felt thick, like I needed fresh air.

I looked into the living room. Bitsy had draped herself over the arm of a sofa, and she laughed as Kyle held up a quarter and wiggled his fanny.

"Demonstration, anyone?" he drawled.

Pammy was nowhere to be seen.

The next morning, I called Phil and told him to meet me at Memorial Park. He showed up with a ratty blanket, two king-sized

Cokes, and a milk-carton box of Whoppers, my favorite candy. Obviously I'd sounded more depressed than I'd intended.

"Hey," he said, putting down the food and spreading out the blanket. As usual, the air smelled foul, because sewage run-off had contaminated the bordering creek. But the park itself was lush and green and nearly always deserted.

Phil patted the spot beside him. "Take a load off."

I sat down and accepted one of the Cokes. The rattle told me he'd gotten extra ice, just the way I liked it. "What's better than roses on a piano?" I asked.

"Exsqueeze me?" Phil said.

"Tulips on my organ," I said. "Hysterical, huh?"

Phil wasn't there yet.

"Tulips on my organ," I said again. "Two lips on my—"

He winked and pointed his finger at me. "Clever girl. You make that up yourself?"

"Parker Rylant told it at the party last night, one of many blow-job jokes. You should have been there."

"Wasn't invited," Phil said.

"L'Kardos got steamed, because he said he didn't want Keisha to hear that kind of crap. He said it was sexist and offensive."

"And right he was," Phil said.

"Absolutely," I said. I sucked on my straw, remembering Keisha's expression when I'd laughed, before I realized the joke was in bad taste.

Phil stretched out and propped his head on one elbow. "Tell me more."

"They were like princesses," I said. "Fairies. And everywhere they went, they sprinkled their magic fairy dust and made everyone adore them."

"And 'they' would be . . . ?"

"Who do you think? Keisha and Bitsy and Mary Bryan." I reached for the Whoppers. "Bitsy told Ryan Overturf she'd have to slap his ass if he didn't give her a foot rub, and Brad, Bitsy's boyfriend, just laughed like *Haha, that Bitsy, such a joker.* And then Ryan was rubbing his thumb up and down Bitsy's instep, and Bitsy was purring and arching her back, and the whole time Brad was turning redder and redder. So finally Bitsy said, 'Be a doll and get me another mojito, will you, Brad?' And Brad snapped out of it and said, 'Sure, Babe. Anything you want. Ryan, need another Coors, man?'"

"That's so lame," Phil said.

"I know."

"Don't they know that friends shouldn't let friends drink bad beer?"

I shoved him. "Anyway, they were total goddesses, and I was a floundering blob of patheticness."

"You're not a floundering blob of patheticness."

"Yeah, right."

"You only are when you say you are, so stop saying it."

"Whatever." I paused, remembering Nate Solomon's complete obliviousness to my very existence. Except my crush on Nate was one thing I would never bring up in front of Phil. So I told him about my inglorious retreat instead.

"I hid behind the island in Kyle's kitchen, because everyone I tried to talk to ran screaming for the hills," I said. "*Now* am I a floundering blob of patheticness?"

"Ouch," Phil said. He looked startled. "Did anyone see you?"

"No."

"Well, thank god."

"You think?"

He plucked a piece of grass. He threw it over the edge of the blanket. Then he circled back to the embarrassment at hand and said, "You hid behind the island? Why didn't you—I don't know—camp out in the bathroom or something? Or better yet, why didn't you just leave?"

"And how would have I done that? Bitsy was the one driving, remember?" I fiddled with the Whoppers carton, opening and closing the top like a fish mouth. Inside, the malted milk balls gleamed. "Ohhh, and get this. Bitsy came in while I was hiding there, and I about had a heart attack."

I told him what happened, how she blasted Pammy Varlotta, and he winced at all the right places.

"It was horrible," I finished. "Even when it comes to cut-downs, Bitsy's a notch above."

"And this is a good thing?" Phil asked.

"You say it like it's not."

"Well, is it?"

I put down the Whoppers. I had a feeling I wasn't going to be able to explain this. "Listen. If Pammy had wanted to insult some-one, what would she say?"

"I have no idea."

"She'd say something ridiculous, like, 'Ew, where'd you get your shoes—Kmart?'"

Phil waited.

"But Bitsy's more . . . subtle." I saw what flickered in his eyes, and I said, "All right, so maybe not subtle. More like sophisticated. Smart. I don't know."

"Cruel?" Phil suggested.

"Maybe. I never said she wasn't." I squirmed. "Jesus, will you stop looking at me like that?"

"I just don't get why you'd want to be friends with her, then."

"Hey, better her than Pammy Varlotta."

He arched his eyebrows. I glared.

"You are really annoying me," I said.

"What? I didn't even—"

"Anyway, Rae says we have no choice. She says we have to like them, it's like witchcraft or something. And you yourself said you wouldn't throw Bitsy out of bed, now didn't you?" I jabbed my finger at him. "Ha. Ha!"

"Rae, as in Alicia's sister Rae? She said it's *witchcraft*?"

"You act like it's so bad, to want to be popular. 'Ooo, she wants to be popular. Ooo, she's so shallow.' But—"

"Hold on. Who said anything about—"

"—but *everyone* wants to be popular, whether they admit it or not. And fine. I do, too. So hate me, all right?" He protested, but I railroaded over him. "But it's more than that. Because Sukie Karing is popular. Pammy Varlotta, believe it or not, is popular."

"And your point would be?"

"My point is that it's not about being in the 'in group,' which is so stupid I can hardly believe I just said it."

"Then what's it about?"

I started to answer, then at the last instant decided maybe I didn't want to. "I can't explain."

"Try."

"No. It's unexplainable."

"You started it, so you have to finish it," he said. "It's the rule."

I narrowed my eyes. He widened his, like, *Hey, this one's not my fault.*

"Fine." I lifted my chin defiantly. "It's not about being popular. It's about . . ."

"Spit it out."

"Being one of them."

"The Bitches."

"That's right. And maybe it's not a good thing, but it's what I want." I re-grabbed the Whoppers and popped one into my mouth. It crunched in a really wrong way, and I tongued it back out. "Ew! *Ew!* What the fuck?"

The crushed Whopper, which should have been dense with malt, was practically hollow. First came a layer of chocolate, then a layer of pale brown malt, much thinner than it should have been, and then—

Bugs.

Nearly microscopic, except I could see them moving. I screeched and flapped my hand, and the malted milk ball went flying.

"Holy crap," Phil said. "There were *bugs* in there. Did you see?"

"It was in my *mouth*!" I cried. "Of course I saw!"

Phil whistled. "Like maggots or something. Holy cannoli."

I licked my arm to scrub my tongue. I took a sip of Coke, swished it furiously, and spit it out.

Phil shook the carton of Whoppers. "Are they all like that?"

"Throw them away," I said. I pointed to the heavy-duty trash-can by the water fountain. "Throw them away *now*."

He tipped the carton, and a glossy malted milk ball rolled into his palm. "Relax. I'm not going to *eat* it." With his teeth, he split the Whopper open. He peered at the halves. He leaned closer, then made a strangled sound and flung them into the grass.

"I think I'm going to throw up," I groaned.

"But don't you want to know how they got in there?" Phil asked. He fingered another Whopper, rotating it to study the chocolate glaze. "I don't see any burrow marks or anything." He bit into it and spit the two pieces in his hand. "Hey, hey—we've got a winner!"

The malt core was intact, two pale brown moons. He tossed the halves into his mouth and chewed.

"Phil! Just because you didn't see any bugs . . . just because . . ." I whacked him. "They could be dormant, you idiot!"

He shook another Whopper into his hand and split it open. He examined it. Threw it over his shoulder. "Bad," he pronounced.

"Okay, whoa," I said. "You are getting used to this way too quick."

He checked the next Whopper. "Bad again. I swear, I don't know how the little wormy things get in there." He cracked open another. "Ooo, this one's for you."

I swatted his hand and sent the pieces flying.

"What did you do that for? That one was perfectly good!" he exclaimed.

"I thought I was telling you about my night from hell," I said. "About how inadequate I felt."

"You don't feel inadequate around me, do you?" Another Whopper passed his test, and he gobbled it down.

I cradled my head in my hands, because no, I didn't feel inadequate around him. What I couldn't tell him was that no one would *ever* feel inadequate around him, and that wasn't necessarily a good thing.

He put his hand under my chin. He tilted my head. He looked at me in this serious way, and for a second it was really freaky, because the air pulsed between us and I thought, *Shit, is he going to kiss me?*

"Here," he said, raising a halved malted milk ball to my mouth. "No bugs."

Later I thought about how it was that Phil, like Camilla, wasn't all ga-ga over the Bitches. He thought they were hot, sure, but he didn't fall under their spell like the rest of us. Camilla, she was above it all. At least that was my take on it. But Phil was immune for a different reason: because he was pure. That was a funny word to use on a boy, but it fit. He was pure of heart.

On Monday, I avoided the Bitches as best I could. I picked different routes when I glimpsed any of them in the hall, and I stayed away from the bathrooms altogether. But I ran into Mary Bryan as I was heading for history, and for a moment we were face to face at the bottom of the stairwell.

"Jane," she said.

My stomach dropped, and I pushed into the crowd. She called after me, but I pretended I didn't hear.

At noon I bought a Nutrigrain bar from the vending machine and snuck to the library. I took the long way past the basement art rooms, because hardly anyone except the art kids went down there. A group of them leaned against the wall by the Ceramics Studio. One of them was Raven Holtzclaw-Fontaine, from Kyle's party. I could tell she didn't have the vaguest clue who I was.

In the library, I chose the farthest back carrel. I slit open my bar and got out my book. Ramona was cross because she had to clean up her room, and Beezus was cross because her mother wouldn't let her spend the night at Mary Jane's. Even Picky-picky, the cat, was cross. Cross, cross, cross.

"God, you are so predictable," Alicia said, clomping across the floor. She dragged over a chair from the next carrel. "And thanks for returning all my calls. Really, it meant a lot to me."

"Sorry," I said. "I was busy."

"Yeah, right. Doing what, hiding beneath your covers? I've seen you today, running around like a scared chicken." She tilted her head. "Guess they didn't pick you, huh?"

"Guess not."

"You must have really bombed at the party."

"Guess so." In my mind, I saw Bitsy's expression when she dropped me off. How her eyes hadn't even registered me.

Alicia blinked. For a moment she seemed uncertain, and then she reclaimed her usual brusqueness. "Well, it's their loss," she said. "Let them have their freaky black magic—we're better off without it." She spotted my paperback and grabbed it by its spine, losing my place. "Ramona books again? Jesus, Jane. When are you going to grow up?"

She meant it as a tease, as in *You're so dumb, but I love you anyway.* I snatched back my book.

"Hey," she said. "Just because they didn't pick you doesn't mean you can take it out on me."

"Are you done yet? I need to eat my lunch."

She glanced at my untouched Nutrigrain bar. "Yeah, because you're starving, I can tell." But she stood up. "Not to, like, mess up your whole self pity thing, but are you still going to come to cheerleading tryouts this afternoon?"

I sighed. "Yes. I'll be there."

She gnawed on her thumbnail. "I'm not going to make the squad. I don't even know why I'm bothering. But at least we can be losers together."

I felt really, really tired. "You never know," I said. "Maybe there'll be a miracle."

Sadly, Alicia sucked. I wasn't saying that to be mean. But she just wasn't cheerleader material.

Her voice screeched when she yelled, "Go, Devils!" And during a complicated knee-slap-clap combination, her tongue snuck into position under her lower lip. And her final cheer didn't end with a split. It ended with a squat. And no matter what the group leaders had said, it wasn't okay. Of the sixty-five girls who tried out—over half the girls in our freshman class—only Alicia and Tina Burston failed to do a split. And Tina Burston had a broken leg. She auditioned without her crutches, which was actually pretty impressive. She'd painted her cast green and white.

"I sucked," Alicia muttered as everyone exited the gym. "Don't bother lying, because I know I did."

"Results will be posted tomorrow!" called one of the group

leaders through cupped hands. "But remember, you're *all* winners! Way to go!"

"Yeah, right," Alicia said. "Five of us will be winners, and the rest will be big, fat losers." She pushed through one of the heavy double doors. She didn't hold it open for me, and it caught me on the forearm. I jogged to catch up.

"Aren't you going to say anything?" she demanded without turning around. "Aren't you going to tell me how terrible I was?"

"You weren't terrible," I said. I struggled for something positive. "Your outfit rocked. You really stood out."

She snorted.

"It did. And you can wear the board shorts at the pool this summer. They'd look great with, like, a white tankini."

"Is that my sympathy prize? 'You didn't make the squad, but at least you can wear your board shorts again'?"

"Come on. You don't *know* you won't make the squad."

Alicia strode to the bottom of the concrete stairs that led to the gym. Saabs and BMWs lined the campus drive, and car doors slammed as girls climbed into their rides. Alicia wrapped her arms around her ribs.

"What about when I squatted at the end of 'Pump It Up'?" she asked. "Was it totally obvious I didn't do a split?" Her gaze slid sideways to gauge my reaction, and my heart went out to her.

"It looked fine," I lied. "It looked totally natural."

She kicked at the curb. She wanted to believe me, I could tell.

A car horn played "Dixie," and Rae leaned out of the window of her Plymouth Cougar. "Alicia!" she called. "Let's go!"

Alicia grabbed her bag. She almost met my eyes, but not quite. "Well, see you tomorrow."

"See you," I said. I scanned the line of cars for Mom's Volvo, but she wasn't here yet. Out of habit, I checked for the Bitches. No need. Like Alicia had said, they were way beyond cheerleader-cool.

When we got home, Mom threw her keys on the counter. "Chinese?" she suggested.

"Sure," I said. I didn't care.

She dug the menu out of the junk drawer. "Go ahead and chill out for a while," she said. "I'll call you when it gets here." She waited until I was halfway up the stairs, then stepped into the hall. "Oh, and a package came from your dad. I left it on your bed."

I stopped. I turned around.

"He sent me an elephant hair bracelet," she said. "Not exactly my style."

"An elephant hair bracelet? Is that what he sent me, too?"

"You'll have to open it. I have no idea." She hesitated, and for a second I thought she might say something real. Instead, she flashed me a smile and returned to the kitchen. Several seconds later, I heard, "I'd like to place an order to go, please. What? Sure, no problem."

I trudged back downstairs, because no way was I dealing with

Dad now, even in the form of a boxed-up gift waiting in my room. Already the mention of him had stirred up the familiar mix of anger and loneliness. Anger that this was what he thought being a dad meant, sending knickknacks from all over the world. Or rather, anger that he thought he could get away with it—or was willing to get away with it—regardless of whatever father truth he actually believed in. That was what made it so bad. Because at some level, he had to know he was hurting me. And yet he did it anyway.

Dad used to love me. He would come to my room when I was scared, and he would turn on the light to show me that every-thing was okay. "It's the same house in the night as it is in the day," he'd say. Then he'd sit on the edge of my bed and rub my back until I fell asleep. Even if it was the middle of the night, he'd yawn and stick it out.

I couldn't figure out what had happened to that love, and that's where the loneliness came in. Stupid, pointless loneliness. I fought against it, but it came in anyway, carving me out and leaving me empty.

I went into the den and signed on to the Internet. I checked my e-mail. There was a note from Phil about *Survivor: Senior High*, which he was also addicted to. It would have made me laugh if I'd have been in a better mood. And there was already a moan-and-groan message from Alicia about her cheerleading tryout. "IM me!!!" she wrote.

Maybe later. I could still hear Mom puttering in the kitchen, so I opened a new window and Googled "snarky bitches," since I'd never actually checked the site during my early religions class. At *SnarkyBitches.com*, I learned that if I ever got a boyfriend—not likely, but just say—and he cheated on me or hit me or got a super bad mullet haircut, I could post the sordid details on the site and my snarky sisters would send me all their love. And if I included his e-mail address, they'd flame him with hate messages, up to a hundred a day.

Good to know, but not related to my Bitches.

"My" Bitches, who were not my Bitches anymore.

Before bed, I steeled myself and opened Dad's gift. Inside was a genuine jade hair comb. It said so on the enclosed slip of paper. I unwound the bubble wrap and regarded the comb, which was decorated with inlaid stones in the shape of a butterfly. It was very cute. Only, I didn't do "cute" anymore. Hadn't for years.

I shoved the comb into the drawer with the Egyptian teddy bear. "Thanks, Dad," I said aloud. "It's just what I wanted."

The next morning, as I was on my way to check the cheerleader postings, I saw Stuart Hill pin Camilla Jones against her locker. Just as Camilla didn't kowtow to the Bitches, she also didn't kowtow to the football players, and from the looks of it, Stuart wasn't pleased.

"I hear you've been complaining to Coach Sloan," Stuart said. His ruddy cheeks looked like a little boy's. "I hear you've been talking trash about me."

"Leave me alone," Camilla said, pushing against one of his arms. She gave him her toughest glare.

He reached down and pinched her nipple, right there in the hall. Camilla gasped and drew her arms to her leotard.

Stuart smirked. "Don't go whining about something unless you want it," he said as he sauntered off. "Slut."

Camilla's face flamed. "Asshole!"

I didn't know what to do. My body had frozen when he first started in on her, and now my heart was whamming away, but the rest of me still couldn't move. Camilla's eyes found mine.

"You saw, didn't you?" she demanded. "You saw what that asshole did?"

"I . . . I—"

"You have to come with me to tell Mr. Van Housen."

Oh, crap, I thought. I was a lot better at being nice to Camilla when it didn't involve going public. "I don't think . . . I mean, I don't know what I would . . ."

"You *have* to," Camilla said. She blinked back tears. "Please."

In the office, Mr. Van Housen put down a brochure picturing a scruffy tomcat glaring from within a cage. "Trap, Alter, Release," read the caption beneath the photo. "The Race to Outpace."

He listened impassively as Camilla told her story. "Uh-huh," he said. "Uh-huh, uh-huh." He was using his broken record technique, where he let a student get it all out while not saying anything in response. "Hmm. I see."

"He touched my *breast*!" Camilla said. "That's sexual harassment!"

"Hmm. Well, it certainly is a matter of concern." Mr. Van Housen propped his elbows on the table and touched his fingers together. "You were there?" he said to me. "You saw this happen?"

I shifted my weight. I could tell he didn't like Camilla, and it made me nervous. I hated it when grown-ups went along with the whole social code set up by the students, fawning over the popular kids and treating the underdogs like shit. At the same time, I knew what Mr. Van Housen wanted me to say, and I could feel that pressure weighing on me, too.

"Um, the thing is, I wasn't really paying attention," I said.

Camilla's head whipped toward mine.

"But, yeah," I said quickly. "He did . . . what she said."

Mr. Van Housen frowned. "Yes. All right. Well, Camilla, you can rest assured that the matter will be taken care of."

"Will there be a hearing?" Camilla demanded. "Will he be expelled?"

"The matter will be taken care of appropriately," Mr. Van Housen said, with a look that shut Camilla up. "I appreciate your bringing this to my attention."

I scurried out of his office. When Camilla came out two seconds later, her face was splotchy. She saw me and blanked her expression, but not before I'd seen what was underneath. She ducked her head and hurried past.

At the other end of the hall, the cheerleading results were posted on the community bulletin board. I took a breath and headed over.

"Oh my god!" I heard Tina Burston exclaim. She clapped, and her crutches fell to the floor. "It's a dream come true!"

Two other girls squealed and hugged.

"Where's Kim?" one of them said. "We have to find her. Kim! *Kim!* You made it!"

I pushed my way through the crowd and scanned the list. Kim, Stacy, Rebecca, Tina, and . . . Shelly Clarkson.

Oh. Right. It wasn't as if I were surprised, but just for a moment, I'd thought *maybe.*

I found Alicia at her locker.

"I don't want to talk about it," she muttered. Her eyes were rimmed with red.

"Okay," I said.

"Anyway, who was I fooling? I didn't even want to be a cheer-leader. Cheerleaders just exist to make other people feel bad. Plus, they're stupid."

"Okay."

She slammed her locker and headed down the hall. I walked beside her. At the door to her classroom, she stopped. She stubbed her pink-and-gray All-Star against the hall carpet.

"Rae's singing karaoke tonight," she said. "Want to go?"

"Sure," I said.

She clamped her lips together. She nodded once, then went into the room.

Mary Bryan trapped me after French. "We need to talk," she said.

Sweat popped out in my armpits. "I'm sorry I was such a dork at Kyle's party," I said. "I didn't mean to embarrass you guys."

"What are you talking about?" Mary Bryan asked. "You didn't embarrass us."

"But I was such a loser."

"Well . . ." She shrugged. "I had a great time. So did Keisha and Bitsy."

"Oh."

"Yeah. So don't worry about it." She ushered me down the hall and out the back door of the building. "There's Bitsy. Let's go."

"Huh? Go where?"

Mary Bryan tugged me across the parking lot. She climbed into the backseat of Bitsy's car and scooted over to make room for me. Keisha was already in the front.

"But . . . it's sixth period," I said.

"So?" Bitsy said.

"So I'm supposed to be in LIFE."

She looked at me blankly, and I said, "Learning Inspiration from Empathy. LIFE. Today we're taking a field trip to the zoo, to talk to an expert on feral cats."

"Why?"

"So we can learn more about the cats on campus. So we can learn to coexist, and help other people to—"

"I think you should pass," Bitsy said. "I'm sure the cats will understand."

I glanced back at the building. Then I squeezed into the car.

We followed the winding campus road that led to the back gate, but no one explained what was going on. We left the school grounds, and Bitsy selected a song on her iPod.

"Uh . . . where are we going?" I asked over the music.

"My place," Bitsy said.

"Why?"

"Why do you think?"

A shred of hope sliced through me. Was it possible I was still being considered?

Idiot, idiot, idiot, I scolded myself. *Don't even go there.* I didn't ask any more questions.

The neighborhood Bitsy lived in was even ritzier than Kyle Kelley's, and her house was unnervingly gorgeous, with vaulted ceilings and gleaming hardwood floors. Mary Bryan disappeared into the kitchen and returned with Diet Cokes, pitas, and hummus. I sat on a white leather sofa across from the others, and I crossed and recrossed my legs. On the glass coffee table sat an ornately painted vase. I could hear the ticking of a clock.

"We brought you here to tell you that we're interested in you," Keisha said at last.

"Not to be blunt, but we don't have much choice," Bitsy said. Keisha shot her a look of warning, and she added, "Of course we adore you, it goes without saying."

"Oh yeah?" I said. I tried to form my mouth into a smile.

"It's true," Mary Bryan said. "Out of all the candidates, you're our top pick. It was unanimous."

"Candidates?" I said.

"Chelsea Campion had potential," Mary Bryan said, "but her dad's this Hollywood mogul type, so she's got all sorts of contacts already. She doesn't need us."

"She certainly needs something," Bitsy said. "Her bum's as big as a bloody buffalo's."

"And we almost asked Lynn Seigler," Mary Bryan continued, "but we decided she's *too* pretty. She looks like a model, practically."

She continued listing girls—as well as why they were axed—and my stomach folded in on itself. Too pretty, too well connected, too smart without being nerdy . . . All of these descriptions sounded like *good* things. I didn't understand what any of it meant.

"Carrie Beale came this close," Mary Bryan said, holding her finger an inch from her thumb. "But then we were like, *Ohhh. She doesn't* mind *being a free agent.* Which made us realize that she wouldn't want it bad enough."

"Want what?" I said.

"Do *you*?" Keisha asked. "Even after Kyle's party?"

"What, to be a Bitch?" I tried to play it cool, but my words tumbled over themselves. "Yes. God, yes!"

"Enough to do whatever it takes?" Keisha pressed.

"Well, sure," I said. *They offered a sacrifice, and the sacrifice was accepted,* came a voice in my head. I faltered. "I mean, I think so . . . but what do you mean?"

Mary Bryan got up from her sofa and moved to sit by me. "Don't worry, Jane. You don't have to do anything you don't want to. Anyway, we're not talking, like, bank robberies or kidnapping innocent children."

"But we're not talking a new hairstyle or a cute new pair of boots, either," Keisha said. "Jane's entire life would change. She needs to know that."

Mary Bryan made a face, like *Don't mind her, she's being such a grown-up.*

Bitsy put down her Diet Coke. "I think you're both forgetting the point of being a Bitch, which is to dump your grotty old life and start over again. So of course Jane's life would change. That's what it's all about." She stood and walked to the entertainment center, where she opened a wooden door to reveal a large-screen TV. She pivoted to face us. "Get comfy, dearies. I think it's time for our video presentation."

The video was of Mary Bryan, only I don't think Mary Bryan knew it was coming, because she turned pale when the images flickered onto the screen. "Oh my god," she kept saying. "Oh my *god.*"

It *was* pretty creepy. Someone (Stuart Hill?) had videoed a rafting party that I guess happened last fall, because the Bitsy in the tape had a short, flippy haircut that now had grown out. She was there along with Keisha and a bunch of other kids, all piled onto big rubber rafts stocked with coolers. One of the rafts had a keg floating along behind it, tied to the raft so it would stay cool in the river.

Bitsy was wearing a turquoise bikini, and she looked fantastic. Keisha was wearing a black one-piece, and *she* looked fantastic. They both laughed and sipped their drinks while the other kids drooled all over them. Just like at Kyle's party. A third fantastic-looking girl was there, too, and after a moment of confusion I deduced that she was last year's senior Bitch, now graduated and out in the real world. She was stretched out on the rim of the main raft, wearing cut-offs and a red halter. While I watched, a guy dipped his fingers into his cup and sprinkled beer on her tummy. She shrieked and swatted him, and the guy turned about a hundred shades of happy.

The camera jerked around a lot, so it was hard to see everything. Mainly Stuart stayed focused on Keisha, Bitsy, and the red halter girl, but occasionally he'd pan in on a guy belting out a burp or drumming his chest like Tarzan.

And every so often there'd be a glimpse of Mary Bryan.

It made my heart hurt to see her. She had on a hot pink one-piece made to look like leather, and it was cut too high on the legs and too low in front. Physically I guess she looked pretty much the same as she does now, only it didn't seem that way at all. Part of it was how she held herself, with her stomach held in super tight and her chest sticking out. And part of it was the way she clutched her Styrofoam cup and ripped off the top in little bits. But mostly it was her expression: bright, bright smile even though no one was talking to her. Desperate, shiny eyes.

My thighs felt heavy. Was that how I came across at Kyle's party?

On the tape, Mary Bryan adjusted her bathing suit. She stood in the raft and wobbled toward a junior named Chase Mattingly, then dropped down beside him. Her drink sloshed onto his leg. He glanced at her, annoyed, but kept talking to his buddy Steve. Several times Mary Bryan opened her mouth to speak, but each time she chickened out. Finally she leaned forward so that her breasts practically fell out of her suit.

"Um, you're on the soccer team, right?" she asked.

Chase broke off in the middle of his sentence. "Yeah. Why?"

"Just . . . you're really good," Mary Bryan said. "That was terrific how you scored all those goals last weekend."

"Thanks," he said. He noticed her cleavage—it was pretty impossible not to—and with some sort of guy code, he got Steve to notice, too. "What's your name again?"

"Mary Bryan," she said.

Chase draped his arm around her shoulders. Stuart, who was getting it on film, zoomed in close. To someone else he said, "Hey, bro, check out the titties!" The Mary Bryan on the raft couldn't hear, but the four of us at Bitsy's could.

"Tell you what," Chase said, all pals-y and smooth. "Find me at the picnic area, after we get off the river, and I'll go over the highlights with you. Sound good?"

Mary Bryan's face lit up, and for a second, she looked like the Mary Bryan I knew now. "Okay. Sure!"

The camera jiggled and panned back to the other raft. Keisha and Bitsy were squealing and drawing up their legs while two guys wrestled each other for the tap of the keg. Drops of beer landed on the camera lens.

"Geronimo!" one of the two yelled as he pushed the other overboard.

"Hold on, Mike," Stuart called. "The Stu-Man is on the way!"

The image shook, followed by a blip of static. The screen went blank.

\~

"That was my tryout," Mary Bryan said after what seemed like hours. She didn't meet anyone's eyes. "I didn't . . . I had no idea . . ."

Keisha studied the sofa cushion. Bitsy gazed at Mary Bryan. Her expression was unreadable.

Mary Bryan laughed shakily. "Can we burn it, please?"

Bitsy strolled behind her and stroked her hair. "Don't be a ninny. How else would we prove how far you've come?"

"Why would we need to?" Mary Bryan said. "I'm serious. Can we please burn it?"

"We should certainly burn that bathing suit," Bitsy said. "Wretched."

Keisha stayed serious. "Tell Jane the rest."

Mary Bryan's cheeks went from red to redder. "Oh, let's not. I mean, god. She probably already hates me." She turned to me. "You do, don't you?"

"No," I said. "Of course not!" I wanted to hug her. I wanted to go back in time and make the rafting trip go away.

"If you don't, I will," Bitsy said.

Mary Bryan looked like she might cry.

"Actually, it's okay," I offered. "Whatever it is, you don't—"

"Just get it over with," Keisha said.

Mary Bryan looped a strand of hair around her finger. "It was an accident. I'd had too much to drink." She drew her knees to her chest. "I'd really rather not . . ."

"She and Chase had sex on top of a picnic table," Bitsy said. "Lovely, yes?"

I saw it in my mind—Mary Bryan, Chase, the picnic table—and I wished I hadn't.

"We weren't, like, right out in the middle of everyone," Mary Bryan said. "It wasn't like everyone could see."

I nodded. I gave her my best imitation of a smile.

"I'd had too much to drink, that's all. And it was dark. And honestly, I didn't even . . ."

"We all make mistakes," Keisha said.

"That's right," Mary Bryan said.

"And we learn from those mistakes and become better people," Bitsy said in a singsong voice. She snorted. "Either that or we get fixed, which is infinitely more effective."

"Huh?" I said.

"Nothing," Keisha said. She shot Bitsy a look.

"We *are* going to tell her, aren't we?" Bitsy asked. "She's this year's lucky winner, after all."

I knew something was going on between them. It's not as if

my brain passed over it. And it's not as if I passed over the whole Mary Bryan thing, either. But I latched onto the phrase "this year's lucky winner," and my blood pulsed faster. I had the brief thought of asking about Sandy—Had they heard of her? What did *they* know?—but I knew I wouldn't. It would complicate things unnecessarily.

Keisha stood up and began collecting Diet Coke cans. "Our decision's not final until tomorrow." She glanced briefly at me. Almost as if she were apologizing, she said, "We had to meet with you one last time. You understand."

"Sure," I said. "Okay."

"So we'll let you know."

"Great. Sounds good."

I hesitated, then got to my feet and helped clean up. As I was collecting Diet Coke cans, Mary Bryan approached me.

"I'm not that girl anymore," she said.

"I know," I said, because I got it. Mary Bryan had changed, and I wanted to, too.

Bitsy took me home, with Mary Bryan and Keisha in tow. We stopped at Steak and Shake for dinner, which surprised me, but I didn't complain. A few other kids from school were there, too. Sukie Karing. Josh Barnett. I tried to act nonchalant, but I was puffed with pride that I was the one entering with Keisha, Mary Bryan, and Bitsy. Sitting at their table. Sharing their conversation.

"Double cheeseburger, fries, and a Sprite," Bitsy said when our waitress approached. "No, strike that. Chocolate shake."

"Whipped cream?" the waitress asked.

"Hell yeah," Bitsy said. She looked at the rest of us. "What? A girl's got to eat."

"Right, which is why your fridge is stocked with pita bread and Diet Coke," Mary Bryan said. I could have been wrong, but it seemed like a bit of a payback.

"Hey, that's my mum's food," Bitsy said.

Mary Bryan made a face. "Hate pita bread."

"So shove it up your ass," Bitsy suggested.

"The rest of you know what you want?" the waitress asked.

We ordered. As soon as the waitress left, Sukie Karing slid out of her booth and came over to ours. Her eyes lit briefly on me—curious, I could tell—but it was Keisha she directed her comments toward.

"Oh my god. Did you hear? About Mr. Cohen?"

Keisha lifted her head.

"What happened?" Mary Bryan asked.

Sukie gripped the edge of the table. "He might have *rabies.*"

"What in bloody hell are you talking about?" Bitsy said.

Now Sukie focused on Bitsy, almost as if she'd been waiting for permission. "He got scratched by one of those cats. You know, at school? It was curled up under his jacket on a sofa in the teacher's lounge. He reached for his jacket to put it on, and the cat went nuts and attacked him. I'm not kidding."

"You were there, were you?" Bitsy said. "You saw it with your own two eyes?"

"No, but everyone's talking about it. He got scratched all down one arm. He had to go to the hospital."

"I don't think you can get rabies from a cat scratch," Mary Bryan said.

"Well, maybe not rabies," Sukie said. "But it's like, those cats are a total menace. What if it had been a student who got scratched?" She leaned forward and spaced out her words. "Total. Law. Suit. City."

"Lawsuit city," Bitsy repeated. She shared a glance with Keisha. "Hmm."

"One chocolate shake, two Sprites, one water," our waitress said. "Now, who had the water?"

Sukie stepped to the side, edged out by the tray. "Anyway, it's just really terrible, that's all. Poor Mr. Cohen."

Bitsy accepted her shake and took a sip. She smiled up at the waitress and said, "Do you think I could have an extra cherry? If it's not too much trouble."

"I'll bring you a whole cupful," the waitress said. "How's that sound?"

"Marvelous," Bitsy said.

Sukie nibbled at her fingernail. "Well. I guess I better go back. I just wanted to let you know."

"Right, then," Bitsy said. "Thanks for the chat."

"Oh, sure. No problem. All right, well . . ." She raised her hand. "Bye!"

"Ta!" Bitsy called. She waited until Sukie was gone, then shook her head. "Ah, Sukie."

Mary Bryan giggled.

I fiddled with my straw. "I've gotten scratched by a cat millions of times," I said, "and I've never gone to the hospital."

"Bingo," Bitsy said. "And that, luv, is one of the many reasons we picked you and not her."

"Huh?" I said.

Bitsy winked, and I did the *ha-ha, very funny* thing. A tingling warmth rose inside me.

The waitress returned with a plastic condiment cup filled with cherries. Bitsy selected the shiniest one and popped it in her mouth.

Three messages waited for me at home, all from Alicia. "Jane, pick up," came the first one. "We're leaving in fifteen minutes." Then came, "Jane! Where are you! Karaoke, remember?" And finally, "You better not have blown me off. I mean it. We'll swing by your house just in case—you better be there!"

I leaned against the counter. Crap. Guilt knuckled down inside me, along with frustration at the unfairness of it. I *hadn't* blown her off. I'd honestly forgotten we had plans. But I knew she'd be pissed regardless.

Ah, shit.

I picked up the phone, knowing it would only be worse if I left it until tomorrow. Plus, if I called her now, she wouldn't be there.

She'd still be at the karaoke bar, nursing a Coke and her indignation.

"Hey, Alicia, it's me," I said after the beep. "I am so sorry. I don't know what's wrong with me, I swear. I fell asleep in the library, can you believe it? I'm a total loser, I know. So anyway, hope you had a great time. See you tomorrow!"

I still had the taste of french fries in my mouth. It was making me thirsty.

The next day I made a point of getting to my locker way early so that I wouldn't run into Alicia, and I managed to dodge her between classes as well. After French, I met up with the Bitches. Me and Mary Bryan and Keisha and Bitsy. They didn't say anything to me, just, "Right, let's go." When we got to Bitsy's, it was like total déjà-vu. Same empty house, same white sofas. Although this time we had Perrier and soy nuts, so it wasn't completely the same after all.

I sat down on one sofa, and the three of them sat across from me on the other. I twisted my fingers in my lap.

"You know why you're here," Keisha said.

I did, but I wasn't so dumb as to say it out loud.

"We're very careful whom we pick to join us," she said, "and we're impressed with your qualifications." She ticked off points. "You're a freshman. That's essential, of course. You're not in any remedial classes. Your looks meet the minimum requirements."

"Which is to say you're not a dog," Bitsy said. She winked.

"But mainly, we like your attitude," Keisha said. "You appreciate what we represent, and we know you'll make us proud. Am I right?"

"Um, yeah," I said.

"Because we'll be investing an enormous amount of energy in you, Jane. You'll have to work hard to be worth it."

I felt silly, but I nodded anyway. "I will. I promise."

Bitsy leaned forward. "And everything we tell you remains secret. Do you understand?"

"Of course."

She arched her eyebrows. "Once you're in, you're in. It's a forever kind of thing, luv. So think about it before you give your answer, because you better be one-hundred-percent sure."

I gazed at their faces. They all looked so serious. Mary Bryan smiled encouragingly, but she was gripping her Perrier harder than she needed to. For no good reason I thought of cats. Of black magic and girls who were dead. Fear twanged in my stomach, and I had an out-of-body sensation of standing over a pit, about to fall in.

Don't you dare, I told myself. *Don't you dare wimp out now.*

"I want in," I said. "I want to be a Bitch."

Time stopped. And when nothing happened, I had a moment of panic. *Is that it?* I thought. *What happens next?*

Keisha picked up her backpack from the floor and withdrew a small box. She walked to my sofa and stood in front of me. I stood, too.

"In that case, we ask you to be one of us," Keisha said. "Do you accept our invitation?"

Hokey, whispered a voice inside me, but I embraced it, because hokey was better by far than the other.

"I do."

"And do you swear to keep all our proceedings secret and confidential, or face the consequences?"

"I do."

She opened the box and took out a key. It was dull with tarnish. She placed it in my palm and folded my fingers over it.

"This is your key," she said. She gave me a meaningful look, but I didn't know what the meaning was.

"Okaaay," I said. I felt its weight and wanted to open my hand and look at it. But I didn't know if I was allowed.

Keisha's expression softened. "Congratulations."

For no reason, my eyes filled with tears.

"Oh no," Mary Bryan said, "now you're going to get me going, too!" She jumped up and hugged me. "This is so awesome, Jane! You're one of us!"

"For real?" My lips wobbled into a grin.

Bitsy unfolded herself from the sofa. She strolled to the kitchen and returned with a bottle of champagne. She popped the cork, and foam bubbled out.

"Cheers," she said. "You're officially a Bitch."

speak

The fly, the fly. The fly in the ointment. The fly in the ointment was this: The key Keisha gave me was to Lurl the Pearl's private office. Not her classroom, where she held office hours and gave tutorials, but a separate office in Hamilton Hall. And the Bitches had instructed me to go there with an item from the girl whose popularity I was willing to suck away, because for me to rise, I had to knock down someone else . . . or something like that. My memory of Keisha's instructions was more than a little muzzy. But anyway, only then would I become the Jane I was meant to be. Uber-Jane, with bonus molecules of charisma bouncing from my cells.

It was crazy, of course. Crazy enough to make my skin prickle. Although of course I'd hidden my reaction.

I had slept hard after yesterday's induction ceremony, but

this morning I replayed it all over again. How Keisha had explained the rules with a straight face, and how she frowned when I kept giggling. But I couldn't help it. It was either giggle or fall into the pit, and I chose to giggle. Because it made me feel better . . . and because by that point I'd had two glasses of champagne.

"So it's like an initiation," I'd said. "You want me to steal something from someone to prove I'm, like, loyal."

"It can be a Chapstick," Mary Bryan said. "Or a ribbon. It doesn't have to be something big."

"But it's not to prove your loyalty," Keisha said. "Like I said, it—"

"Close enough," Bitsy intervened. She smiled to show that she knew Keisha was going a little overboard. "Jane gets the picture. Right, pet?"

I didn't, because I refused to. "The thing is, there's really no need, because I'm totally yours already," I said. "So we can skip the rite of passage dealie, okay?"

Keisha looked pained. Bitsy blew air our of her cheeks. She went to replenish the soy nuts. Mary Bryan bit her lip, then grabbed the bottle of Veuve Cliquot Grande Dame and topped off my glass.

"The thing is, you kind of have to," she said. She grimaced, like, *I know it sucks, but what can we do?* "I know it's a drag. I do. But it's not like we want you to *hurt* anyone. Like I said, you can take something so small it doesn't even matter. A Lifesaver, even."

"Can I just ask someone for one?" I said. I could do that, ask whoever for a Tootsie Roll or a stick of gum.

"No, you have to take it," Keisha said wearily. "You have to pick a girl, someone different every week, and take something that belongs to her—"

"*Steal* something that belongs to her," Bitsy said. She'd returned with more nuts, which she picked through with one hand. She widened her eyes at Keisha's scowl. "What?"

Keisha turned back to me. "And then you have to deliver it to Lurl the Pearl. If you want to be one of us for real, that's what you have to do."

"Ohhh," I said. The giggles started up again. "So let me see if I'm getting this. I'm 'officially' a Bitch, but I'm not officially a Bitch until I pass the test. Is that it?"

"You have to steal something and give it to Lurl," Keisha repeated.

"But why Lurl the Pearl?" I said, remembering how she scolded me for my Internet hanky-panky. "Anyway, she'll turn me in. Unless she doesn't know the thing isn't mine, in which case she'll be like, 'Why is this freak giving me her Chapstick?'" I covered my mouth with my hand. "Oh my god, she'll think I'm hitting on her."

Mary Bryan sighed.

Bitsy wiped salt from her fingers onto her jeans. "This is getting extremely old."

"Well, what do you suggest?" Keisha said. "If she doesn't come through, you're screwed, too, you know."

Mary Bryan leaned back on the sofa so that her head was resting on the cushion. She stared at the ceiling. "It's been a long summer," she said. "I feel like I'm changing."

"Well, you're not," Bitsy snapped.

"That's what I tell myself, but . . ." She lifted her hands, then let them drift back to the sofa.

"Oh for crap's sake," Bitsy said. She put down the bowl of nuts and stood before me. "Look, Jane. You'll take someone's bloody Chapstick and you'll give it to Lurl. Got it?"

"Bloody Chapstick," I said. "Ick. Bad image."

"Unless you're afraid to," Bitsy said.

I grinned. This was classic. "Afraid? *Moi?*" I went mock-solemn, pressing the tips of my fingers together in prayer. "Just tell me one thing. You guys aren't going to make me kill a—" I almost said "cat," but changed the word at the last second. "A dog, are you?"

Mary Bryan shot a swift, startled look at Keisha.

"Of course not," Keisha said sharply.

Mary Bryan trained her blue eyes on me. "I love dogs," she offered. "I wish I could get one, but my mom won't let me."

Bitsy studied me. I couldn't read her expression. "Come on, luv," she said. "Throw us a bone."

I downed the rest of my champagne, which really was delicious. Like fat yellow bumblebees. "Oh o*kay*. As long as I don't have to kill a dog to get it."

Bitsy half-smiled, then selected a soy nut from the bowl. She held it, but didn't eat it. "Quite the dark horse, this one, isn't she?"

I buzzed with pleasure, as if she'd seen the secret me. Uber-Jane, ready to take on the world.

But today, as I trudged to my locker, the giddiness was gone. In its place stirred an unsettling confusion. Because hahaha, great joke and all that, only they'd never broken character. Not once. No smirks to show it was all a game, no shared looks when they thought I wasn't watching. They were good, those three. Either that, or . . .

No. A girl couldn't really siphon away someone else's popularity. Could she?

It didn't escape me that Lurl the Pearl did, in fact, have a sideways connection with all that was spooky. Her early religions course, for one, with its focus on age-old rituals and mythologies. And she herself was weird as hell.

Then again, if the Bitches wanted to shroud themselves in mystery—while at the same time putting me through the paces— then Lurl was the obvious choice. I'd read more than just Ramona books, and I knew how this stuff worked. The crusty old man in an antique store; the wizened librarian with owlish features; the pale, silent comic-book collector living forever in his parents' basement—this was the stuff that rumors were made of. Lurl the Pearl was Crestview's creepiest option, and of course the Bitches were willing to take advantage.

That didn't mean I wanted to give her a stolen offering, though. But what choice did I have if I wanted to be accepted by the others?

Through my headache, I noticed all the shit girls lug around every day. Lipsticks, cell phones, compacts. Little plastic makeup pouches attached to the loops of backpacks. Clippies shaped like butterflies. Jewel-studded barrettes. Tubes of body glitter. Gum.

But I couldn't actually *steal* anything from anyone. For starters, someone was sure to see. Her eyes would lock with mine, and I'd yank my hand from her backpack, leaving the body glitter behind. "Sorry," I'd say with a burning face. "I was just wondering what kind it was."

I twisted the dial on my lock. Beside me, Sally Howarth's locker stood open while Sally chatted with Leila Hobbs. Sally had decorated the inside of the door with colorful magnets, some holding up pictures, but some on their own, serving no purpose whatsoever. Just wasting space.

Sally fished around for the notebook on top of her stack of books. She slammed her locker and headed down the hall with Leila.

"You look like hell," Alicia informed me, pulling off another of her great sneak-ups. "Seriously. You look even worse than I do."

I whipped around, my pulse in overdrive. "Gee, thanks," I said.

"I'm just being honest."

"Uh-huh. And thanks again."

She leaned against the lockers on my other side. She'd trimmed her bangs, and they lay in a straight, black line over her eyebrows. "Anyway, if you're worried that I'm still mad at you, I'm not. Which I would have told you if I could have found you at school yesterday. Or if you ever answered your damn phone. You're like this lady of the night now, always off on some mysterious adventure. What's up with that?"

I closed my eyes. I needed to tell her. *Had* to tell her. But I knew she wasn't going to like it. I opened my eyes. "Um, actually I—"

"Yeah, whatever," she said. The hall was filling up, and some guy knocked her off balance as he passed. "Meet me in front of Hamilton after math, all right? I've got big news. Bigger even than cheerleading. See you!"

Okay, then, I thought. Saved by the bell, which hadn't yet rung. I shoved my French books into my backpack and closed my locker. I scanned the floor, hoping to spot a wayward pen. A paper clip, even.

But there was nothing there.

"I know, I know, it's totally out of character," Alicia said two minutes into our free period. "You're thinking, 'Who is this chick,' right? 'Who is this girly-girl who's taken over my best friend's body?'" She widened her eyes. "But Jane."

"But *Alicia*," I said.

"He is amazing," she said. "I'm telling you, I've never had a crush this bad."

"You've never had a crush, period."

"Because there's never been anyone worthy. Until now." She nodded, as if to suggest that yes, it was incredible, and yes, she could handle it if—understandably—I didn't know how to respond.

I *didn't* know how to respond, but not for the reason she suspected. I'd spent all of math class gearing up to tell her about the Bitches, and the strategy I'd come up with was to spill the news in a great excited burst, as if I fully assumed that she'd be as happy about it as I was. No room for wounded resentment, that was the goal.

But now here was Alicia, telling me her own news in a great excited burst. She'd morphed into an actual human being—happy, even—and I'd barely been able to get a word in edgewise.

"So are you going to tell me who he is?" I asked.

She gripped the cement bench we were sitting on. "Tommy Arnez. We got put in the same group for English—how lucky is that?" She lifted her eyebrows. "And you know how much I hate group work."

"But not anymore?"

"Not anymore. No sir, no way." Her voice went dreamy. "Tommy Arnez."

"Ah," I said. Tommy Arnez was a drama geek, not a super-cool jock or a hottie in a garage band. Tommy's friends called him

"Babyface," because of his big, round face that matched his big, round body. He was way talented, and I wouldn't be surprised if he ended up on Broadway someday. But he was the funny guy, the always-joking guy, not the smooth-moves-and-aftershave guy. Which was good, because it meant Alicia had a chance.

"Ms. Morgan assigned us this asinine project, which was to come up with five 'essential learnings' for the semester," Alicia said. "We were all like, 'You're the teacher. That's your job.' But Ms. Morgan said we had to take ownership of our own experience—gag, gag—and that after coming up with the essential learnings, we had to decide what would happen to anyone who didn't learn them. And you know what Tommy said?"

"Tell me."

"'Throw 'em in the chokey.'"

"The chokey? What the hell is the chokey?"

"That's what I said, too!" Alicia said. She slapped the bench. "He said it's, like, this dark closet with sharp nails sticking out all over the inside. Like a medieval torture chamber, kind of." She smirked. "Ms. Morgan was not amused."

Apparently, Alicia was.

"And get this," she said. "Are you ready?"

"I'm ready."

"We left class together, and we talked all the way to our lockers. And then last night, he called me up and invited me to this fundraiser thing on Saturday night. It's for this performance art group called Howling Muses, and they do all this hilarious stuff like put poems into tampon dispensers." She whapped my leg, a series of rapid pats. "Can you believe it?"

"Alicia, that's awesome."

"I know!"

"I am *so* happy for you." I upped my smile and barreled ahead. "And guess what? I have good news, too. I'm a Bitch!"

"Huh?" Alicia said.

"You know, a Bitch. A *Bitch*. They picked me after all!"

Alicia's face muscles slackened, and for a second I saw the old Alicia shining through. But she covered her jealousy almost immediately. "Oh my god. Jane, that's fantastic!"

"Really? You mean it?"

"Of course I mean it. Why wouldn't I mean it? What kind of friend wouldn't mean it, you spaz?"

To her credit, she was really trying. And her own windfall softened the blow, I'm sure. Gladness bubbled through me, and I decided just to run with it. She was happy for me, and I was happy for her. Why should that be too good to be true?

"So . . . when did this happen? And how?" Alicia asked. "Tell me, tell me, tell me."

So I did, and it was so nice not to have to edit myself and make it sound less mind-blowing than it really was. I skipped the part about the stealing, however, because that was privileged information. Besides, it wasn't a detail I needed to share.

"In-freaking-credible," Alicia said after I'd finished and after I'd answered her many questions. She tilted her head, going for supportive with a dash of caution. "You've just got to promise to be careful, okay?"

"Yeah, of course. But there's nothing to worry about, Alicia."

"I know," she said. "I'm just saying."

A warmth radiated between us that I hadn't felt for a while. We grinned at each other.

From the building came the muffled ringing of the bell. Kids poured from the doors. I saw Phil trip and go sprawling, and I saw Stuart Hill behind him, slapping John Rogers's palm. I instinctively started to rise, even though I was too far away to help.

"Shit," Alicia said. "I wanted to make myself beautiful for English." She unzipped the bottom compartment of her pack and fumbled for her mirror. "Do I look okay?"

A girl named Oz Spencer stopped and gave Phil a hand, and I sat back down on the bench. Oz was chubby, with hot-pink hair, and she had a tendency to wear low riders that showed her butt crack. I liked her for being nice to Phil.

"You look fine," I told Alicia.

Alicia scrunched her hair, then rubbed her teeth. Her backpack drooped off the bench, and keys and makeup clattered to the ground.

"Fuck, I don't have time for this!" Alicia cried.

"Relax," I said. I knelt to retrieve her junk, thinking anew how lucky I was to be me instead of Oz or Phil or Alicia. My fingers closed over a tiny tub of lip balm, which I shoved into my pocket. The rest I scooped into her pack.

"You're the best," Alicia said. She snatched her backpack and slung it over one shoulder. "Bye! Wish me luck!"

"Good luck!" I called as she hurried up the sidewalk. "Give him a kiss for me!"

I grabbed my pack and headed for French. Below my hipbone, the tub of lip balm pressed into my skin. I felt quivery, although I pushed the sensation down as best I could.

It's only lip balm, I told myself. *You've borrowed lip balm from each other a million times.*

Anyway, it was done. There was no point worrying about it now.

Mary Bryan squealed a muted squeal. "Yay," she said, clapping quietly in the crowded hall. "The hardest part's over, I swear. And at least you didn't throw up like I did. I honestly threw up, that's how nervous I was." She took the lip balm and turned it over. "So whose is it?"

"Um—"

"Never mind, I don't want to know." She returned the lip balm, a quick hand-to-hand transfer. Her eyes were shining. "Now all you have to do is get it to Lurl. Easy-peasy, right? That's what Bitsy says."

Easy-peasy. Right. I wedged the lip balm back in my pocket.

"I was actually thinking . . . do I really have to give it to Lurl?"

She frowned at me as I were being silly. "Uh, *yes*, Jane. That's kind of the point."

"But why?"

"*Because.* That's the way it works."

I sighed. I wanted to push further, but something held me back.

"Well, will you at least come with me?" I said. "I wouldn't ask, except I'm afraid I'll mess up. Or that I'll run into Lurl and not be able to do *anything*, because if I have to actually talk to her, I'm pretty sure I'll lose it. I mean, what would I say to her? 'Here, I stole this for you'?"

"You don't have to say anything," Mary Bryan said. "Just put it on her desk and leave."

"But won't she think that's extremely weird?"

"She'll think it's extremely weird if you *don't,*" she said. I must have looked blank, because she made an impatient movement with her hands. "She knows you're coming. She's expecting you."

"*What?!*"

Mary Bryan stepped closer. She scanned the hall, then lowered her voice. "She's really very nice. She's just . . . shy."

My insides tightened. "You *have* to come with me."

"I don't know. Keisha wouldn't like it."

"Please."

She twisted a strand of blond hair around her finger and pulled the end to her mouth. I scrunched my toes inside my sneakers.

She dropped her hand. "Okay, but we have to do it *now.* Can you be late to your next class?"

I nodded.

"Then come on," Mary Bryan said. She led me to the third floor of Hamilton Hall, where we strode past a half dozen classrooms, including the room where Lurl taught her early religions class. Then she turned right down the south hall. Yellow and black police tape blocked the entrance to the English Department lounge, site of Mr. Cohen's cat attack.

"Idiots," Mary Bryan muttered. An empty metal cage sat outside the door, a fuzzy pink and turquoise ball lying in the corner. Mary Bryan kicked the cage as she passed. The ball jingled as it rolled to the other side.

"This way," Mary Bryan said. She tugged open the heavy door at the far end of the hall. The door led to the dim corridor that connected the south hall to the north hall. Since it didn't open into any classrooms, it wasn't highly trafficked. Its walls weren't even plastered with the requisite charcoal sketches and pastel self-portraits of various art classes.

I held the door and paused outside the corridor. I remembered something from Rae's ghost story, about how the sacrifice was made in an abandoned storage room on the third floor of Hamilton Hall. Off a hall that nobody used.

Mary Bryan turned around. "Jane? We're almost there. Come on."

I buried the memory and quelled my uneasiness. Or tried to, anyway. I joined Mary Bryan, and the door swung shut behind us. We walked a couple of yards farther and stopped in front of Lurl's office. I knew from the fake wood placard held in place by two metal clips. S. L. LEAR, it said in flaking gold letters.

"There," Mary Bryan said, jerking her chin.

I stood there. A terrible dread stole through my veins, and this time it got the best of me. *They offered a sacrifice, and the sacrifice was accepted. They offered a sacrifice, and the sacrifice was accepted.*

Mary Bryan glanced at the end of the corridor, at the closed door that led back to the main hall. "Go ahead. Use your key."

"I don't want to."

"You *have* to."

I inched toward the door, then drew my key from my pocket and fit it into the lock. A noise came from the main hall, and both of us jumped. I met Mary Bryan's eyes.

"Go," she said.

I pushed open the door, realizing with a too-late jolt that I should have knocked first. Oh god, why didn't I knock?

But the office was empty. Mary Bryan hurried me in and shut the door behind us. She flicked on the light, and the shadowy form of a desk and filing cabinet sprang into resolution. Nothing else.

"This is it?" I said.

Mary Bryan crossed her arms over her chest as if she didn't want to accidentally touch anything. Not that there was anything to touch. The office was completely sterile.

"Well, yeah," she said. "What did you expect?"

I exhaled, my fear diminishing. Now I felt silly for feeling scared in the first place.

"It's, like, dead in here," I said. "Are you sure she even uses it?"

"Just put the lip balm on the desk and let's go," Mary Bryan said.

At the far end of the office was a second door. I moved toward it, asking, "What's in there? Is there another room connected with this one?"

Mary Bryan grabbed my arm. "You're not allowed."

I sniffed, catching a whiff of something vaguely meaty. "Hey. Do you smell cat food?"

"No. Put the lip balm on the desk."

"I totally smell cat food. Oh my god, do you think—"

"What I think is that I took my own time to come here with you, and now it's really uncool that you're making me late to class," Mary Bryan said.

"Oh," I said. "I just thought . . . I mean, we're already late, so . . ."

"It's just extremely inconsiderate."

I flinched. I'd never seen Mary Bryan pissed before. I didn't think she got pissed. I wiggled Alicia's lip balm out of my pocket and approached Lurl's desk. Then I stopped short, my body going cold. On the corner of the desk was a dead kitten, its tiny head lolling unnaturally from its body.

And then it was just a pencil sharpener. A gray mechanical pencil sharpener, its handle jutting out by its base.

My breath rushed back. A layer of sweat slicked my skin. I set the lip balm on Lurl's desk and stepped away.

"Thank you," Mary Bryan said. She strode out of the office and waited while I pulled the door shut and locked it. We walked without speaking down the corridor, and it wasn't until we were back in the main hall, past the water fountain and a bright mural of a teeming jungle, that she relented.

"Sorry I snapped at you." She gave me a sideways look.

"No, *I'm* sorry," I said. I gave her a sickly smile. I was still recovering from my fright. "I didn't mean to make you late, honest."

"Yeah, well. Madame Herrera's going to kill me anyway. It's not like five minutes are going to make a difference."

We stopped at the top of the stairwell. Her class was back on the first floor; mine was two doors down.

"So whose was it, now that it's done?" she asked.

"Whose was . . .? Oh, you mean the lip balm?"

She nodded.

I paused, then spit it out. "Alicia's. Alicia Dugger's."

Mary Bryan paled.

"I know," I said. "I know, I know. But it's not like she's never borrowed anything from me before. I'll get her a new one, I swear."

"But Keisha told you," Mary Bryan said. "She didn't keep anything secret, she told you right up front . . ."

"You mean that hocus-pocus from last night?" I said. I tried to laugh it off. "Come on."

Mary Bryan twisted the bottom of her shirt. "She told you how it works," she whispered. "'For one to rise, another must fall.'"

It brought the cold feeling back to my body, and I almost felt as though I was going to faint. "Please. You guys are nuts. I mean, it's done, okay? I did what you wanted, so you can drop the whole charade thing."

She gazed at me.

"Because it's really pretty stupid," I said. It was the first time I'd said anything like that to her, anything the slightest bit critical.

But all Mary Bryan said was, "Don't do it again. Not if she's your friend." She touched my arm, or rather the cloth of my shirt. She turned and hurried down the stairs.

During geometry, something odd happened. I was taking notes as Mr. Hopper explained some proof when suddenly the world slid sideways. My pen clattered to my desk, and a shimmer pulsed through me. Life was an infinite web of lights—I knew it because I felt it—and mine burned brighter than most.

The sensation lasted only a second, and then it was gone. I was still me, my butt on the hard plastic seat. But I understood, although I wasn't sure how, that Lurl had found the lip balm.

At lunch, the cafeteria lady handmade my turkey sub, adding guacamole, fresh tomatoes, and two strips of caramelized bacon. I put aside thoughts of offerings and rituals and gave myself to the moment.

"How did she know?" I asked Keisha, glancing down the food line to verify that yes, the lesser mortals were receiving Turkey

Joes. I spotted Phil receiving his plate, and he grinned a hello. He motioned with his eyes at Keisha, a gesture that meant, *Someone's moving up in the world, hmm?* Then the cafeteria lady handed him his Turkey Joe, which was gray, and he turned back quick not to drop it.

"Chill," Keisha told me under her breath. "Never act entitled."

"So *here's* our starlet," Bitsy said, joining us as we exited the line. "This way, luv. We're sitting with the cheerleaders today. Fair's fair, you know, and Elizabeth positively begged."

"She did?" I said.

"We try to keep a clean rotation," she explained. "A little taste for everyone."

At the cheerleaders' table, I sat between Bitsy and Keisha and across from Elizabeth, Amy, and Jodi, who drank me in with wide eyes as if they'd never seen me before. Which, although they had, they probably really hadn't. Mary Bryan sat two seats down, fawned over by Laurie and Trish. She lifted her hand in a wave.

"Oh my god, this is so exciting!" Elizabeth said. She rapped her plate with her fork. "Everyone, this is *Jane*. Jane, this is everyone. Jane's the new . . . you know!"

"No way," said Amy. "Congrats!"

"That's awesome!" cried Jodi.

"How do you feel?" asked Elizabeth. "Are you thrilled? You must be so thrilled!"

Bitsy leaned in, murmuring, "I for one bloody well am.

Haven't felt this grand in weeks, you brilliant girl." She hooked me with her arm and grinned at the others. "She's superb, yeah?"

"She's just precious," Elizabeth affirmed.

I blushed from my head to my feet. The only other conversation I'd had with Elizabeth had ended with "Who the fuck are you?"

"I . . . you know. I'm really happy," I said.

Jodi reached over and grasped my chin, the way a grandmother might do. She squeezed it and let it go. "Oh, she is just too darling for words."

I couldn't stop smiling. And why not? Yesterday I was nobody, but today I was precious, darling, superb. A tiny part of me way back in my head said, *Wait. Hold on. Can this really be?* But it was squashed by the coos of the cheerleaders, who weren't—I was absolutely sure—faking their adoration. Because I had never felt anything like this before, these waves of positive regard. It was like being bathed in love.

They bombarded me with questions: What music did I like, where did I get my T-shirt, did I want them to do my hair? I answered dizzily. I giggled and tilted my head. A few tables over one of the feral cats yowled and took off with the turkey from someone's sandwich, and Jodi put on a very serious face.

"I'm sorry you had to see that, Jane," she said.

"Huh? Oh, that's okay," I said. "I'm used to it."

Jodi blinked. "Don't you think they're a nuisance, though? Don't you think something should be done about them?"

After a quick glance at Mary Bryan, I said, "Actually, um, I think everyone should just leave them alone. I mean, they're not really hurting anybody, are they?"

Jodi drew back. She changed her expression to reflect this new perspective. "That is so mature. Live and let live, right?

Amy and Laurie nodded their support.

"We should start a petition," Trish suggested. "What do you think, Jane? Maybe hold a pep rally?"

"We could dress up like kittens!" Jodi said.

Elizabeth held out her hand. "Not me. Uh-uh."

"Why not?" Jodi asked.

"The whole squad? Out there prancing around for everyone to see?"

"It would be cute."

"Uh, *no*. It would be demeaning."

Bitsy spoke into my ear. "Silly cows."

I looked away and smiled.

"I think a pep rally is a good idea," Keisha said. "It would be a great way to raise awareness."

"See?" Jodi said, jabbing Elizabeth.

"And I know you all will figure out the best way to stage it," Keisha went on. "That's what you do. That's why y'all are the cheerleaders."

Jodi lifted her chin. They all sat up a little straighter.

"But right now we need your help with something else." She touched my shoulder, and I sat up straighter, too. My skin hummed with specialness. "We need to plan a party for Jane. Will Saturday night work for everyone?"

"I'll be in charge of decorations," Amy said right away.

"And I'll do food," said Jodi. "I have an *excellent* recipe for flaming custard in individual spongecake boats."

"Where will we have it?" Laurie asked. "Should we invite guys?"

Keisha stood up, and Bitsy and Mary Bryan followed suit. I quickly got to my feet.

"Thanks, girls," Keisha said. "We know we're in good hands."

"Just don't bring the megaphones this time, eh?" Bitsy said.

We left them talking excitedly. I hadn't eaten a bite of my food, but I wasn't the least bit hungry.

In English, Miriam Fossey looked at me funny and nudged her best friend Angel. She and Angel whispered back and forth, and Angel's eyebrows shot up. Then Angel whispered something to Bobbi, who passed it onto Taniqua. Soon all the girls in the class were whispering, and I knew it had to do with me. I knew because after class, Miriam made a point of coming over and talking to me, which she hadn't done all year.

"There's something different about you," she accused.

"There is?"

"I saw you at lunch. You were sitting with Bitsy and Mary Bryan and Keisha."

I tilted my head. In fifth grade, Miriam and I had been friends.

We both liked to swing. Then in sixth grade, she told me my neck was dirty. That was soon after Dad had left. She said she couldn't hang out with me anymore, that her mother had said so.

"Huh," I said to her now. "So I was."

Miriam scrunched up her mouth, and I could tell she was dying to say something snotty. But what was there to say? Anyway, Miriam was a snob, but she wasn't stupid.

"Well," she said at last. "Lucky you."

On Friday, we ate with the debate team. Boiled chicken breasts for them, Duck à l'orange for us. I had never tasted duck before. It was delicious.

However, the debaters weren't as fun as the cheerleaders. They were at first, when they told me how wonderful I was using phrases like, "as evidenced by your superior mental endowment" and "proven without contest by your taste in dining companions." But then they fell into an argument about the importance of peer group interactions, and it got really boring.

"Why?" moaned Bitsy as Rutgers Steiner pressed Callie Winship about the multiple definitions of "social intercourse." "Why, why, why?"

"Just tune them out," said Mary Bryan. She plucked a marinated orange slice from my plate. To me she said, "The stoners are even worse. All they do is gaze at us and stroke our hair."

"So why do you—" I made a *dumb me* face. I started over. "So why do we bother? Why don't we sit with whoever we want?"

"Yes, Jane," Bitsy said. "Excellent question." She turned to Keisha. "Why don't we?"

Keisha telegraphed her disapproval. "Because it wouldn't be fair."

I waited for more. Bitsy rolled her eyes. Finally, I said, "Oh."

"At least we get to be together," Mary Bryan said. She appropriated another orange. "You know, the four of us."

I scooped the remaining orange slices from my sauce and slid them onto her plate. "Here."

She grinned. "Thanks."

Bitsy nudged my elbow. "What's this, pet? A friend of yours come to visit?"

I glanced up to see Alicia walking toward us with a wavering smile. I looked beyond her at the drama table. Tommy Arnez was shaking his head, his face flushed. His friend pushed his shoulder and laughed.

"Hi, guys," Alicia said in a wobbly voice. "Can I sit with you?"

It was the first time I'd been around her since the lip balm incident, and I was hit by an unreasonable annoyance. No, she couldn't sit here. She should go back to her own table where she belonged.

But I said, "Uh, sure. Of course. But . . . why aren't you sitting with Tommy?"

"He's helping Bryan rehearse his lines for *Our Town*," she said. "I didn't want to mess them up."

"Lovers' spat, eh?" Bitsy said. She seemed perkier than she had all meal.

"No," Alicia said. She pulled her chair in beside me, so close that her leg brushed mine. I inched my chair farther to the left.

"But something's going on," Bitsy said. "I can tell."

Alicia hesitated, then blinked two times. "We've got a date for tomorrow night."

"Do you now?" Bitsy exclaimed. She selected a French-cut green bean and waved it in the air. "Go on."

Alicia started telling us detail after pathetic detail, all in a nasal, wheedling voice, and I squeezed my napkin into a ball. Gone were the warm fuzzies from our chat outside Hamilton, replaced with an urgent desire for Alicia to shut the hell up and stop embarrassing me. I knew I wasn't being fair—this was Alicia, not some toad, slimy with need—but I couldn't help it. I didn't want her touching me.

"But it's not like you're a *couple*," I said.

Alicia blushed. "I never said we were. I said we have a date, that's all."

"Yeah, but it's, what, to some performance-art thing?"

"So?"

"So?" I laughed. If she would have let it go, then I would have, too. But no. She had to ooze in where she wasn't wanted. "You said that part of their act involves a tampon dispenser."

Her blush deepened. "I told Jane she was going to change if she hung out with you all," she said. "And now she has. She's just acting this way to impress you."

"Oh please," I managed. My face went hot, and I felt blindsided by her disloyalty. "Why don't you tell them what you really told me? How I should stay away from them because they're—" I clamped shut my mouth. I'd almost said "witches." Witches, bitches, I had an insane desire to smack the whine right out of her. I shoved my hands beneath my thighs.

Alicia glared at me. "Anyway, it's for poems," she said. "It dispenses *poems*."

"Poems in a tampon dispenser," Bitsy said lightly. "How clever."

Alicia squished up her mouth, not knowing if Bitsy was making fun of her. And then all at once her shoulders slumped. "It's not like I had anything to do with it," she said.

Mary Bryan's eyes met mine. I knew I should feel ashamed, but I didn't.

"Well, I think it sounds really fun," Mary Bryan said. "First dates are exciting no matter what you do."

"I wouldn't know," Alicia said.

"And if things go well, maybe he'll ask you to the Fall Fling," Mary Bryan went on. "It's only two weeks away, you know."

"The Fall Fling," Rutgers Steiner said, diving back into the conversation. "Now there's an example of authentic social intercourse. Do you agree, Callie, or do dances fall into your category of ritualized teenage cannibalism?"

"The Fall Fling isn't a *dance*, Rutgers," Callie said. "It's an *event*. Which you would know if you had your finger on the pulse of actual high-school dynamics."

Off they spun into another argument. Alicia scooted back her chair.

"Call me tonight?" she muttered.

"Sure," I muttered back.

"Bye," she said to the others. "I didn't . . . I mean, I hope I wasn't . . ."

"No worries, luv," Bitsy said. She smiled breezily and took a sip of Perrier. "I just hope you and Timmy work things out."

"Tommy," Alicia said.

"Tommy. Right."

Alicia took her tray and left.

"Sorry," I said. I glanced up at Keisha, Bitsy, and Mary Bryan, and the rage I'd felt began to drain out of me. Now I felt shaken by my own reaction. "She isn't always such a toad."

Mary Bryan frowned. Bitsy laughed. Keisha said nothing at all.

On Saturday morning I IMed Bitsy for party fashion advice. I was too chicken to call her in person, but I needed her input. Plus, I wanted the thrill of IMing Bitsy McGovern. Of knowing I actually could.

It's your coming-out party, she IMed back. *Wear something sexy.*

So I did. I wiggled into my shortest denim skirt, which I'd bought in a moment of summer madness and had never worn. It covered my crotch and not much more, and if I'd seen it on another girl, I'd have *tsk*ed with jealous scorn. But hell, I had good legs. More importantly, I was a Bitch. The knowledge unleashed me.

"Another party?" Mom said when I jogged downstairs.

"Yep," I said, moving quickly behind the sofa so she wouldn't comment on the skirt. "It's my coming-out party."

Mom looked confused. "What?"

"Nothing," I said. Bitsy's horn beeped from the driveway. "So . . . bye! See you when I see you!"

The party was in an abandoned warehouse that somebody's brother had rented or something like that. I didn't get all the details, and when we got there, I didn't care. It was a huge open space, like a barn, and the cheerleaders had decorated it with strands of silver star lights and red Chinese lanterns. Velvet cushions were piled in the corners, and along one wall sat a gold brocade sofa with dark green throw pillows. A rent-a-hot-tub bubbled away in the center of the room, and a full bar was set up ten feet away. Kyle Kelley held court with a bottle of Tanqueray and a lemon. When he saw us, he raised the bottle in salute.

"It's amazing," I breathed.

Mary Bryan seemed pleased, as if it were a present she was responsible for.

"They did a nice job," Keisha acknowledged. She wore a pale sage dress that matched her eyes, and she looked like a creature from a fairy tale. Compared to her I was a vamped-up club girl, but I hardly cared.

"Knock 'em dead," said Bitsy. She used her thumb to soften

my sparkly eyeshadow, which she'd applied for me in the car. "You're the belle of the ball."

Raven Holtzclaw-Fontaine: I'm just really happy for you. And I'm not just saying that.

Me: Yeah? Hey, thanks.

Raven: Just be careful, that's all. It's so emotional. No matter how exciting it is, it's so emotional.

Me: Uh . . . okay.

Raven: Take me, for example. Like how I got an art scholarship to RISD, right? But I'm not going to let it go to my head, even though it is one of the most prestigious design schools in the country.

Me: You got a scholarship? That's awesome!

Raven: Wow. That is so nice of you to say so. I mean, I thought you might be all full of yourself, but you're not. And I'm not going to be either. Unless I'm forced to.

Me: You'll do great. I know it.

Raven: Listen, do you think I could paint your picture sometime?

Elizabeth Greene: Everyone sees me as just this kick-ass cheerleader, but there's more to me than that, you know? And this internship I've been offered could be the opportunity of a lifetime. Only, a year is a really long time. And Antarctica's friggin' *cold*, there's no getting around it.

Me: That's true. I do think it would be cold.

Elizabeth: Plus there's only this one research guy in the lab I'd
    be working in, and he's ancient. He has one of those tubes
    in his neck to speak with, but apparently he's not much of a
    conversationalist.

Me: Jesus. Don't you think you'd get lonely?

Elizabeth: I think he's self-conscious.

Me: Well, I guess you just have to ask yourself if it's worth
    it or not.

Elizabeth: Oh my god.

Me: What?

Elizabeth: Nothing, you've totally put it in perspective, that's
    all. Because you weren't afraid to take on a whole new life,
    were you?

Me: I never . . . huh. I mean, I guess I wasn't, was I?

Elizabeth, hugging me hard: You're my hero, Jane. I'm
    going to go for it. I am!

Pammy Varlotta: Hey.

Me: Hey.

Pammy: Great party, huh?

Me: Man, it really is. I didn't know parties like this even
    existed—you know, before I hooked up with Bitsy and Keisha
    and Mary Bryan.

Pammy: I know what you're saying. I mean, not that I'm

claiming to be in your shoes or anything. Is it awesome,
being a Bitch?

Me, laughing: God, is that all anyone can talk about? It's
like every single person has to bring it up.

Pammy: But . . . you brought it up, not me.

Me: What? No, I didn't.

Pammy: Yeah, you did. Just now when you talked about hooking
up with Keisha and everyone.

Me: Oh.

Pammy, wistful as hell: You're sooo lucky. And it couldn't have
happened to a nicer person, that's what everyone's saying.

So . . . is it awesome?

It *was* awesome, especially when I steeled my nerves and
approached Nate Solomon over by the bar.

"Um . . . hey," I said, smoothing my skirt over my thighs. If this
Bitch thing was really working—really and truly and not just
pretend—then Nate would respond.

He stayed focused on the task at hand, which was stabbing a
hole into the bottom of his beer can with a pen.

"What are you doing?" I asked.

His eyes strayed to me, and the beer slipped from his hands.
Foam fizzed from the gash.

Mike Miller chortled. "Beauty, man. Smooth move!"

Nate turned red, and my head buzzed with the unrealness of

it. He dropped his beer *because of me*. He was blushing *because of me*.

"Shut up," he told Mike, bending down and snagging the can. He pitched it into the trash.

I giggled, and Nate grinned self-consciously. He wiped his hands on his jeans and stepped toward me. My body tingled.

"You're Jane, right?"

"Yeah."

"You, uh, want to shotgun a beer?" He gestured at Mike, who, having pierced the bottom of his can, was now pressing the hole to his mouth and guzzling away. "When you pop the top, it comes pouring out."

"Oh," I said.

"We have pony beers, if you're not ready for full-size." He ducked behind the bar and produced a beer in a six-ounce minia-ture can. Then he plunked a really big beer beside it, twice the size of a normal beer. "Or we have tall boys, too. Want to try?"

"No thanks," I said. "But I'll watch you."

"Yeah? All right, cool." He grabbed the tall boy, and Mike tossed him the pen. With sure aim, he punctured the aluminum. He drew the hole to his mouth, popped the top, and chugged.

"Rock it!" called Mike.

"Dude!" cheered another guy.

Nate's throat was long and taut as he swallowed. When he lowered the can, Schlitz glistened on his upper lip.

"Ice bonus," Mike said. He strode to the bar and slapped Nate a high five.

Nate wiped his mouth with his forearm, then checked to make sure I'd been watching.

My skin warmed with excitement.

But the best part of the evening came later, after most everybody had left or passed out. Mary Bryan steered me to the back entrance of the warehouse, and we went outside into the cool night air. Keisha and Bitsy, too. Just the four of us. An iron ladder scaled the brick wall, and I followed Mary Bryan when she started climbing.

"Ooo, I can see Jane's knickers," Bitsy said as she climbed up behind me.

"Shut up," I said. Me, to Bitsy. I was heady with glory.

On top of the roof, we leaned against the metal housing of the air conditioning unit and reviewed the evening. Trucks rumbled by on a nearby thoroughfare, their headlights jogging over street signs. Occasionally they made the building shake.

"That was a very good time," Mary Bryan said.

Keisha wrapped L'Kardos's jacket more tightly around herself. "L'Kardos told me he loves me," she said softly.

"Keisha!" Mary Bryan squealed. She gasped and grabbed Keisha's hand.

"Took him long enough," Bitsy grumbled. But she reached

over and wiggled Keisha's knee. "That's fantastic, Keisha. He's dead yummy, and you know I don't lie."

"That's great," I said shyly. I thought about Nate's strong arms, but kept them to myself. "He seems really nice."

Keisha smiled. She rested her cheek against his jacket.

"Well, nothing nearly so exciting for me," Bitsy said. "Keisha gets a big romantic moment, and what do I get? A grope on the sofa and Brad's tongue down my throat."

"Ew," Mary Bryan said.

"Not to worry. I gave him the boot."

"Bitsy!" Mary Bryan exclaimed. "Are you serious?"

Bitsy shrugged. "I'm well shot of him. Anyway, I've got my sights on Ryan Overturf. Talk about yummy. Did you see those trousers he had on?"

"'Those trousers'?" Mary Bryan teased. "Anyway, no, because Pammy Varlotta was using them as a cushion for most of the night. I'd say you've got your work cut out for you, Bitsy my luv."

Bitsy snorted. "What a butter cow."

"Only Ryan really does seem to like her." Mary Bryan giggled. "Guess you'll have to wear a retainer and talk with a lisp like she does. Apparently that's what he goes for."

"Is that why she talks like that?" I asked. "She has a retainer?"

"It's on the inside of her teeth so you can't see it," Mary Bryan explained.

"Don't be mean," Keisha said.

"What? Saying someone has a retainer isn't being mean."

Bitsy stretched, an expansive, hands-over-head movement that pulled her top up to reveal her tummy. She let her arms flop down. "I think I'm up to the challenge of Pammy Varlotta. If not, there are always other ways."

"No," Mary Bryan said, feigning shock. "Don't tell me you'd break your fixation just for the sake of Pammy."

"As I said, I highly doubt it will come to that."

"What are you talking about?" I asked. "What fixation?"

"More like vendetta," Mary Bryan said.

"Could we please not ruin the evening?" Keisha said.

"And did you hear?" Bitsy went on. "Stuart's on probation from football, all because of some ridiculous complaint she made. Pompous slag."

"Who?" I said, totally confused. "Pammy?" Then something clicked in my brain. Stuart, complaint, pompous slag . . . "Wait a minute. Are you talking about Camilla Jones? How Stuart harassed her that one day?"

"What do *you* know about it?" Bitsy asked.

I should have been warned by her tone. Instead, I was glad of the chance to contribute. "Well, not a lot," I said, hoping to sound offhand. "But I was there, that's all. And I went with Camilla to tell Mr. Van Housen."

"So you ratted Stuart out?" Bitsy said.

My stomach dropped. I looked from face to face.

"Um . . . do you guys not like Camilla?" I asked. "Is there something I'm missing here?"

There was a pulse in the air. Mary Bryan's eyes flew to Bitsy, and then she quick-laughed and said, "What? We like Camilla."

"Except when she's a right little prat," Bitsy said. "Which is always." To Mary Bryan she said, "You brought it up, so don't act all innocent."

"Hey, don't put it on me!" Mary Bryan protested. "I have no problem with Camilla. I like her fine."

Clearly, she didn't. Clearly, none of them did. Which baffled me, given Camilla's loner status. I was surprised they even knew who she was.

Then I thought about Camilla some more, how she was the one person who didn't worship the Bitches like everyone else. Was that what this was about?

"Anyway, I didn't rat Stuart out," I said. "I just, you know, said that Camilla was telling the truth. That Stuart did what she said he did."

Bitsy made a derisive noise. Mary Bryan ducked her head and fiddled with her hair. Keisha gazed at the rooftop, but as usual, she didn't speak.

"Camilla was just standing there," I explained. "He pinned her against a locker and . . ." I looked at each of them. "Come on, you guys. It was bad."

Mary Bryan lifted her head. "It's just . . . well, you were kind of right. Bitsy's not really one of Camilla's fans."

I held out my hands, palms forward. "Neither am I, I swear!" I said. As the words spilled from my mouth, I realized they were true. Until this very moment I'd thought I liked Camilla. Sort of. I'd admired her, at any rate, for being true to herself in a dog-eat-dog world. Only now that admiration was gone, replaced with . . . ickiness.

Just like the ickiness I'd felt toward Alicia, that day in the cafeteria.

Oh, shit.

"Did one of you guys . . ." I started. "Bitsy, did you . . ."

Bitsy arched one eyebrow.

I decided I didn't have a question after all. I had a heart-pounding feeling of having done something wrong, although I *hadn't*, so I pushed forward with my story. "Anyway, Mr. Van Housen pretty much blew her off. He acted like she was a huge nuisance."

"Yeah?" Mary Bryan said. She turned to Bitsy, like, *Did you hear? Isn't that great?*

I tried to do better. "She was all whiney, like, 'Wah, wah, wah, poor me.' And Mr. Van Housen was all, 'All right, girls. The matter will be taken care of appropriately.'"

"She's a—what'd you call your friend the other day?" Bitsy said. "A toad. A slimy, bug-eyed toad."

"I know," I said. "I mean, if she would just . . . be less aloof or something. But she doesn't even make the effort."

Bitsy's mouth twisted. "Everything she gets, she deserves."

Mary Bryan stared at her fingernails.

"Next time stay out of her way, right?" Bitsy said.

I nodded. "Sure. Of course."

"And if she gives you any problems, come to me. I'll make sure she doesn't bother you."

"Leave it alone, Bitsy," Keisha said.

"I'll leave it alone when I want to leave it alone," Bitsy shot back.

"Guys," Mary Bryan pleaded.

"What, now *you're* going to get on my back, too?"

"Just . . . stop. Okay? This is Jane's night. We don't want to spoil it with things that don't even matter."

Mary Bryan turned to me and smiled unconvincingly. "Did you have fun? Was it everything you thought it would be?"

"Um . . . yeah. It was awesome."

"For real?" Mary Bryan said. "You're not just saying that?"

I pushed Camilla from my mind, because despite it all, the glow from the night still remained. I wasn't going to let her ruin it. "Well, I don't want to sound stupid, but . . ."

"You won't sound stupid."

I blew out my breath. "It was just really nice, because I think everyone liked me. Even when I acted like an idiot."

No one spoke. It was as if they were letting my words float down around them.

"Yeah," Keisha said at last. "It feels good, doesn't it?"

Mary Bryan leaned against me. She rested her head on my shoulder.

"Well done, you," Bitsy said, her venom gone. "Well done, our Jane."

I dreamed about second grade, when Mom signed me up to be a Junior Bird Girl. We made thumbprint owls and microwaved s'mores. On the last day, to symbolize flying from the nest, we were blind-folded one by one and led into a circle of fellow Bird Girls. I folded my arms over my chest as I was passed from girl to girl, feeling their small hands on my shoulders and back. First they whispered bad things about me: *You're too skinny. You smile too much. You suck at math.* Then came the good things: *I like your barrettes. You're kind to animals. Your hair is so soft.* I remembered their fluttering touch. The sensation of taking flight.

"Hey, Janie-girl. What's up?"

It was Phil, calling way too early the next morning. I held the phone away as I stretched, then brought it back to my ear.

"Hey, Phil," I said. "You woke me up."

"Want to go to Memorial? Have a picnic?"

"Right now?"

"It's eleven o'clock. I'm starving."

"You *woke* me *up*."

"Fifteen minutes, then?"

I rubbed my hand over my face. I arched my back and pointed my toes. "Make it twenty."

I brought the milk. He brought the Krispy Kremes. Breakfast of champions—or in this case lunch.

"So what's kickin'?" he asked, tossing me a still-warm doughnut.

"'What's kickin'?'" I repeated.

"Nate Solomon said he saw you last night at some fancy party." He made his voice sound mocking. "He said you were *hot*."

I tried to hide my reaction, but I couldn't help smiling.

"For real? Are you shitting me?"

"He was like, 'Sorry you weren't there, *dude*. Sorry you're such a loser, *dude*.'"

"Oh, he did not. I think Nate is very nice."

"Apparently he feels the same way," Phil said. "You're the flavor of the season. You're the new black."

"Please."

"Seriously, what's the story?" He licked a smear of glaze from his thumb, pretending he didn't really care, but his eyes gave him away.

I tried to calm down, although inside I was jumping all around. But Phil was not the person to share it with.

"Well . . . I guess it's because I'm a Bitch," I said.

"No you're not. Don't even say that."

"No," I said. "I'm a *Bitch*, like Keisha and Bitsy and Mary Bryan. They ended up picking me after all." I grinned, filled with goofy joy. "Last night was my coming-out party."

"Oh," Phil said. He didn't seem terribly happy. "But in reality you're still plain old Janie. Right?"

"Gee, thanks."

"No, I just meant that Nate's never drooled over you before. So why should he drool over you now?"

"You're kind of digging yourself into a hole, pardner."

"He's never even *mentioned* you before."

I looked down, unsure how to proceed. We were coming close to talking about something that we really didn't need to talk about, and I didn't mean the whole mysterious popularity thing.

I used my sneaker to nudge his high-top. His crappy, tattered high-top. "Come on. Aren't you happy for me?"

"I just don't get why hanging out with Mary Bryan and Keisha and Bitsy would make such a difference." He finished his milk and crushed the carton. "Why does it even matter who you hang out with?"

Oh, Phil, I thought. *You really mean that, don't you?*

I decided to try a different tactic. I let my voice take on a playful tone and said, "Anyway, I've noticed you making new friends, too." I raised my eyebrows. "Oz Spencer? Hmm? Does someone have a little bit of a crush on someone?"

He looked at me as if I were nuts. "Oz? She's in my physics class."

"She's nice," I said.

"Yeah, I agree, but I don't have a . . ." He sighed. "On Friday, Mr. Lesmeister made her tie a sweatshirt around her waist. You could see her thong because her pants were so low, and the guy behind her wasn't getting any work done."

I thought of my failed thong attempt. At least Oz had the guts to go for the glory.

"And were you that guy?" I teased.

"No," he said. "It was Matthew Lyons."

He seemed frustrated, and I felt bad. I let the joke go and flopped back on the quilt.

He lay back beside me. His jeans, super dark like those a cowboy might wear, stretched alongside my just-the-right-bit-faded ones. We gazed at the sky.

"Listen, Janie," he said. "I *am* happy for you. I guess it's just weird having all these other people figure out what I've always known."

I turned my head. "Phil, that is the nicest thing anybody's ever said to me."

He nodded, like *yeah, he knew*. Then he said, "The Fall Fling's coming up."

I got a nervous feeling in my stomach. "Yeah . . ."

"You probably won't want to now that you're, you know, upper crust, but—"

"Phil."

"You think you might want to go with me?"

I blinked. On the one hand, no, I did not want to go with him. I wanted to go with Nate. Not that Nate had asked me, but he could. And now that I was a Bitch, he actually might. Which made me realize—holy shit. Phil had never asked me to anything like this before, so why now? Was he only asking me because I was a Bitch? Even if he didn't know it, was that the deep-down reason?

I didn't like where that was going, and anyway, no. Phil was Phil. He liked me just for being me. As for Nate, well, crushing on him was one thing. The thought of making it real—or taking a step toward maybe making it real—was way too scary.

A decision blossomed within me, and I knew it was the right thing to do. I faced Phil and was floored to see that he'd turned a bright, painful red.

"Phil . . ." I began.

He didn't meet my eyes. "It wouldn't have to mean anything."

"Well, duh. What I was going to say was sure. Let's do it."

"Yeah?"

"Yeah."

I rolled over and gave him an awkward hug. Surprised, he hugged me back.

plainjain: hey, mb. wazzup?
bayBdoll: nmjc. u?
plainjain: normal ol' sunday. i'm avoiding homework and

mom's making fried chicken. mmm.

bayBdoll: lucky u. sunday nite chez moi is pretty much fend-for-yourself nite. then again, so is every other nite.

plainjain: ouch

plainjain: wanna come here?

bayBdoll: that's ok, my brother said he'd make burritos. but thanks.

plainjain: no prob

plainjain: so i was kinda wondering what bitsy's deal is. that is, if ur ok talking about it. if not, that's totally fine.

bayBdoll: about camilla, u mean?

plainjain: yeah

bayBdoll: well . . . it's complicated.

plainjain: oh

bayBdoll: if i tell u, do u swear not to tell bitsy?

plainjain: OF COURSE

plainjain: it's just that she seemed so pissed last nite, like totally out of the blue.

bayBdoll: yeah, well, they have a long history.

bayBdoll: camilla lives in bitsy's neighborhood, did u know that?

plainjain: really? i thought camilla was, like, poor.

bayBdoll: u'd think so, with all her anti-establishment bullshit and those leotards she always wears. but no. she's rich as sin. that's not why bitsy hates her, tho.

plainjain: then why?

bayBdoll: cuz . . . ah, shit. cuz camilla saw something she wasn't supposed to, over the summer.

plainjain: did it have to do with

plainjain: u know

bayBdoll: what?

bayBdoll: OH. no, not that. it was something personal.

bayBdoll: look, i'm just gonna tell u, but like i said, u have to promise not to tell.

plainjain: i promise. u know i do.

bayBdoll: i'm serious. bitsy would kill me.

plainjain: mary bryan, i swear i will never say a word.

bayBdoll: bitsy's dad took off, ok? he ran off with some floozy. and instead of telling bitsy to her face, he stuck a note on the windshield of her car. can u believe that?

plainjain: omg, that's terrible

bayBdoll: only bitsy found the note before he left, and i guess she and her dad had this big scene in the driveway. bitsy lit into him for being such a bastard, and he gave back as good as he got. apparently he said all this stuff about not wanting kids in the first place and how he'd never signed on for changing the nappies of a 16 yr old.

plainjain: jesus. and i thought MY dad was bad.

bayBdoll: anyway, they were both pretty much shouting their heads off, from what bitsy told me.

plainjain: and camilla heard?

bayBdoll: and camilla heard.

plainjain: crap

bayBdoll: she'd walked over cuz of the noise, and bitsy spotted her at the end of the driveway. only here's the worst thing. i guess by that point bitsy had moved from shouting to . . . well, groveling.

plainjain: BITSY?

bayBdoll: hard to imagine, isn't it?

plainjain: forget hard. try impossible. i didn't think bitsy knew HOW to grovel.

bayBdoll: well, "grovel" isn't the word bitsy used, obviously, but that's the sense i got. there were tears involved, i do know that.

plainjain: how?

bayBdoll: cuz when bitsy was telling me about it, her lips got all tight and she said, "but i DIDN'T cry. i NEVER cry."

plainjain: which of course means that she did

plainjain: poor bitsy

bayBdoll: so that's the great drama. i would just steer clear of the whole camilla situation if i were u.

plainjain: no shit

bayBdoll: hey, i gtg. i've got a freakin huge english assignment.

plainjain: yeah, ok. only can i ask one more thing?

bayBdoll: what?

plainjain: that other stuff. the bitch stuff. god, i feel retarded even saying it. but blah, blah, blah, the little stealing ritual and all . . .

bayBdoll: oh god. we're going there again?

plainjain: no. no, never mind.

bayBdoll: jane. r u happy being a bitch?

plainjain: mary bryan! u KNOW i am.

bayBdoll: then don't worry about it. just enjoy the fact that life is good.

plainjain: ur totally right

bayBdoll: of course i am. and now, gbye!!!

One of the feral cats sprayed Alicia's locker. It stank to high heaven, and on Monday morning everyone made "pee-ew" sounds and waved their hands in front of their noses. "Piss Girl," they called Alicia, and it didn't matter that it made no sense.

"What'd you do, Piss Girl?" Stuart Hill taunted. "Leave some chicken guts in there?"

"Shut up," Alicia said. "I didn't leave anything, you asshole."

"Not even your books?" Stuart said. He guffawed as if he were actually being funny. "Not even a chewed up pencil for your nasty old tomcat?"

The janitor shooed them away. He doused Alicia's locker with Odor-Out, aiming his spray nozzle at the slats and seams as well as the smooth gray exterior.

"Wait!" Alicia cried, but the janitor took no notice. When she opened her locker, a sodden spiral slipped to the floor along with her cheerleading Pep Manual. The stench of cat pee wafted into the air.

I strode toward the other end of the hall. I hoped Alicia hadn't seen me, but two yards from the stairwell, I heard her call, "Jane, where are you going? *Jane!*"

My heart felt sick. I let the flow of students carry me forward.

During Algebra I thought of one of my Ramona books, of a scene in which Ramona was doing a kindergarten worksheet. Only instead of "circle cat, cross out bird," Ramona substituted the name of a despised fellow kindergartner, Susan of the boing-y curls. As in, "circle Ramona, cross out Susan."

It wasn't that I despised Alicia—god, no. It wasn't even on purpose, despite the guilt that was making me feel swampy and wrong.

Still, there it was, crazy or not: circle Jane, cross out Alicia.

roll over

S ix, sin, and sorcery," intoned Lurl the Pearl. "All three words come from the same root, which, once celebrated, has now become vilified."

I copied the words into my notebook and tried to convince myself that it was purely academic, her use of the word "sorcery." That she was just going off on her favorite tangent about how female folk healers, drawing on the life force of the goddess, were later denounced as witches. Blah, blah, blah. She'd shown the film *The Burning Times* twice already. She'd quizzed us on the real meaning of the word "wicca," and she'd told us that many women today have formed their own worship circles as a way to create a sacred space. More interesting than Ms. Bainbright's English class, but hardly the stuff of midnight terrors. At least, as long as I didn't connect it with anything else.

Still, when I'd first taken my seat—after dislodging a gray cat with a torn ear—I could have sworn Lurl looked at me funny through her rose-tinted glasses. Then again, she looked at *every-one* funny through her rose-tinted glasses. The T strap on her forehead didn't help.

What had she done with Alicia's lip balm?

A flutter kicked up in my stomach. *Don't,* I told myself. *What's done is done.*

"Yes, Miss Goodwin?" Lurl the Pearl asked, interrupting her explanation of "six" as the number of the creatrix.

I jumped. "I'm sorry, what?"

"You have a concern?"

The rest of the class turned to stare. Friendly stares, *Hi, do you like me?* stares, but stares all the same.

"Um, I don't." I tried to smile. "Doing fine, thanks."

Lurl smiled back. It was a loose, smeary smile that made her face look as if it were coming unhinged. "Then let's pay attention, shall we?"

"Yes, ma'am," I said.

"Hey," Bob Foskin whispered. He'd gotten up from his seat at the front of the room and was now crouching by my desk. *"Hey."*

"What?" I said. "I've got to pay attention."

He leaned closer. "Want me to knock her around for you?"

"Excuse me?"

"Wait for her after school. Give her a scare."

My eyes flew to Lurl, then back to Bob. "You're not serious."

"As a heart attack," he said, crossing himself. "Ganging up on you for no reason. No respect, that's what."

"Oh god," I muttered. Lurl the Pearl was now roaming the room, and I did not want her coming over here. I straightened my posture and scribbled the number 666, along with Lurl's labored analysis that just as six stood for the creatrix, 666 stood for the holy trinity of maid, matron, and crone. That it was only as people grew threatened by female power that the number took on more sinister meanings.

"No thanks," I told Bob. "You better get back to your seat."

"You sure?"

Lurl was two aisles away. One. She paused at my aisle, and my body went stiff. Bob stood up, but he didn't return to his desk. Lurl didn't even look at him.

"Very nice," she said to me in her gravelly voice. "Very nice. But we can never ease up, can we? Not when the stakes are so high."

My scalp prickled. A force radiated from her, something I couldn't describe, and I got the uncanny sense that she wanted to *eat* me. To gobble me right up.

"So we'll have your assignment by the end of the week?" she asked.

My assignment. As in another stolen item—was that what she was talking about? But I was in a classroom with twenty-three other students. She couldn't be.

"What assignment?" Bob butted in. "We ain't got no assignment."

Lurl came up behind me and put her hands on my shoulders. I wanted to jump out of my skin.

"Miss Goodwin is a good little pet," she purred. "Miss Goodwin is earning extra credit."

"Aw, man," Bob complained. "Why don't I know about no extra credit?"

Lurl bent over so that her lips were at my ear. She smelled like tuna. "By the end of the week for best results."

She tightened her hold on my shoulders, then let go.

During LIFE, my entire class surprised me by singing "Happy Birthday" at the beginning of the period. Roly-poly Mrs. Parmigian sang loudest of all, clapping her hands and swaying at the front of the room. When they were done, Tina Knowles walked to my desk with a yellow-and-white sheet cake, one of those fancy ones with edible flowers and candied ribbons. In the center was an airbrushed picture of me. I looked really young.

"Wow," I said. "I mean, wow."

Fifteen faces beamed. Tina nudged Hannah Henderson, who nudged her back. They both looked tickled pink.

"Only, it's not my birthday," I said.

Tina waved her hand. "That's okay. We figured, you know, what were the odds?"

"We just wanted to celebrate anyway," Hannah said. "Who cares when the actual date was?"

"Happy birthday!" cried Arnie Aughenbach.

"Happy birthday!" echoed fourteen others. Hands patted my back and ruffled my hair.

I grinned. "You guys are crazy."

"Heck, it's better than following the lesson plan any day," said Mrs. Parmigian. She waddled across the room to give me a hug. "In LIFE, there's always cause for celebration."

I raised my eyebrows. "So . . . do I get presents?"

"Presents!" Tina exclaimed. "Of course!" She ran to her backpack and pulled out a brightly wrapped box. Other kids dug into their packs and reached under their desks.

"Mine first," Arnie said, plunking down a lumpy package tied with yarn.

"I don't think so," Tina said. She bumped him out of the way. "Jane asked me, remember?"

"Wait," I protested. "I was kidding. I was completely kidding!"

The stack of presents grew on my desk. I tried pushing them back into their owners' hands, but they wouldn't have anything to do with it.

"Open them," Tina insisted.

So I did. I got the new Spayed CD, a pocketknife engraved with my name, a framed picture of Arnie. Four pairs of earrings. From Tina, a sky blue container of stress therapy bath beads ("Not that you need them. What do *you* have to be stressed about? But they're so cool, because the water gets all fizzy when you put them in!"). A leather bookmark, a mauve feather boa. A tiny tub of lip balm.

"Thanks, you guys," I said. I fingered the lip balm, then pushed it behind the boa. "I mean it. I was having a really crappy day—"

"You were?" Hannah said. "Poor Jane!"

"—but you guys totally made it better." I smiled at them, so easy to do because they all smiled back. "And I *love* my presents. Thank you so much."

A chorus of "aww"s filled the air. Arnie gave me a hug, then Hannah did, too. Melina, who was shy, just touched my hair.

"Now cake," Tina announced. "Oh! Shit! And I completely spaced the band! Arnie, run to the hall and see if they're there!"

The cake was delicious. The band, decked out in full red-and-black Crestview regalia, was awesome. In addition to the school's alma mater, they played a fabulous jazz piece composed in my honor, with an amazing solo on the flageolet.

"Have you gotten it yet?" Mary Bryan asked the next morning.

"Gotten what?" I asked.

She looked at me in a not-fun-and-games kind of way. "You know. To give to Lurl."

A sick feeling clutched my stomach. I fiddled with one of my new earrings, which were shaped like tiny doves.

"Do you like my earrings?" I asked. "Hannah Henderson gave them to me."

"Yeah, they're great," Mary Bryan said impatiently.

"My whole class threw me a party. It was so sweet."

"Terrific. And if you want them to *keep* doing stuff like that—"

I cut her off. "I know, I know."

"Then just do it."

"Fine," I said. I sighed and leaned against the row of lockers. I gazed down the hall. "Will this be the last time?"

Mary Bryan snorted, for a second sounding almost like Bitsy. "Hmm, let me think. This'll be the last time until next week. And then that'll be the last time until, let's see, the next week."

"What?!" I said. I vaguely remembered an "every week" clause from the day of my induction, but it was all so blurry.

"Jane. Keisha told you all of this already." She raised her eyebrows. "And it's not just you, you know. We all have to do it, so you can quit acting like such a martyr."

I went back to staring down the hall. I watched a girl try to shoo a feral cat from her locker, where it perched placidly on a thick blue notebook. The cats were everywhere these days. During homeroom, one had coughed up a hairball on Trish Newman's backpack, and rumor had it that a pack of three had killed a swan and deposited the carcass on Mr. Van Housen's desk. Of course, nobody had been there to verify it, and some claimed that Mr. Van Housen had made it up. Still, the fact remained. The cats were getting more brazen.

"Hey," I said. "Once I . . . you know. Will that mean Alicia's off the hook? She'll go back to the way she was?"

"Back to her usual charming self, you mean?" Mary Bryan said.

I faltered. I got the sense that maybe she was being sarcastic, only I wasn't sure. "Well . . . yeah. She's really not that bad when you get to know her."

"Which is why I was the only one who was nice to her, that day at lunch. Which is why you've basically treated her like a leper since the moment you hooked up with us."

The surprise of it tightened my lungs. "But that's because . . . I mean, come on. That's because—"

"Because we're all just walking bags of shit, waiting to unload?"

I drew back. Mary Bryan, I was finding, was not all sweetness and light.

Down the hall, the cat leaped nimbly from the locker onto the girl's shoulders. The girl crouched and cried out.

Mary Bryan watched, then pushed her fingers against her forehead. After a moment, she dropped her hands. "But yeah, Alicia will go back to the way she was." She half laughed. "Cats will stop pissing on her stuff. The world will adore her."

Our eyes locked. Her expression was weary, despite her glittery eyeshadow and rosy cheeks.

The girl stumbled our way, the cat still lodged on her shoulders, and I had to step to the side to avoid being bumped. Before I could stop myself, I snapped at her to watch where she was going.

She halted and turned around. "Oh god, I'm so sorry," she said. "Are you okay?"

"You about made me trip," I said.

The cat meowed, digging its claws into the girl's shirt. The blood drained from her face. She gestured at her back and said, "Do you . . . do you think you could . . . ?"

Irritation mounted inside me. I yanked the cat off her shoulders, using my hand to free its claws.

"Thank you," the girl babbled. "Thank you so much."

"Yeah, whatever," I said. The cat squirmed to the floor with a thump.

I turned to Mary Bryan, but she was gone.

Lunch with the drama kids—no Alicia, where was Alicia?—and then PE. Not my favorite class on the best of days, but today it was horrible. Sure, Coach Shaw exempted me from doing the rope climb, and sure, Anna Maria and Debbie, who were total soccer studs, told me I should try out for the team. Never mind the fact that I sucked at soccer, and that just two weeks ago Anna Maria had shoved me accidentally on purpose with her shoulder during a game of battle ball. I'd gone sprawling, and Anna Maria had hissed, "Stay down, you idiot. Tell the coach you sprained your ankle."

But today they'd loved me. Great. So really, class itself was fine. It was what happened afterward that screwed with my mind.

Everyone except me was changing out of her gym shirt and shorts. I was still in my normal clothes, since Coach Shaw hadn't made me dress out. But I'd filed into the locker room with the others so they wouldn't think I was a snob.

"Hey, Jane," Anna Maria said, pulling a blue-and-white rugby down over her head. "You going to the Fall Fling?"

"Yeah," I said. I lounged against a wooden bench. "You?"

She stepped into her jeans. "Hell, yeah. Jodi's mom is on the planning committee, and she says there's going to be all kinds of cool shit like bungee cords and climbing walls. You *know* I'm going to be there."

"Cool," I said.

"Some of the girls will be, 'Ooo, it's too scary,' 'Ooo, I'll break a nail,' right? It'll be hilarious. But the people who matter will be, like—" She broke off and turned to Debbie, who'd come up behind her. "What?!"

Debbie jerked her chin toward the end of the locker room. Camilla, a towel wrapped around her waist, was heading from the showers to the nearest row of lockers. Water dripped from her hair onto the back of her T-shirt.

Anna Maria's face hardened. "Whore."

"Why is she even here?" Debbie said. "She's not in our PE class."

"Bet she's been using the weight room again, fucking ballerina princess," Anna Maria said. "Stuart Hill can't use it, noooo. But our fucking little Camilla can."

I frowned. The girls' weight room was separate from the boys', which meant that Camilla doing her weight training wouldn't take anything away from Stuart. But I, too, felt a surge of repugnance at the sight of Camilla, and it scared me.

Anna Maria caught my expression. "She's the one responsible for getting Stuart kicked off the team, you know. Lying whore."

I tried to cleanse my impure emotions. "I thought he was just on probation."

"And the crap she told Mr. Van Housen? Lies. Every single bit of it."

"Huh?"

Debbie stepped closer. Looking at me significantly, she said, "We heard it from Bitsy."

My stomach clenched. What had Bitsy told them?

"But, um . . . how would Bitsy know?" I asked. "She wasn't there, was she?"

"Bitsy knows everything," Anna Maria said. "And she's not scared of telling the truth."

"She's not scared of anything," Anna Maria said. "Especially not a slut in a tutu." She took a step toward Camilla's locker. "Come on, Little Debs."

I got a bad taste in the back of my throat, but I followed anyway. It was as if my feet were on some sick sort of auto-pilot.

They caught her unawares. Anna Maria lunged forward and grabbed her towel, leaving Camilla in just her T-shirt and panties.

"Hey!" Camilla cried.

"You think you're so hot," Anna Maria said. "But you're not. Everyone hates you, you slut."

"You're such a lesbo," Debbie contributed. "Prancing around like a freaking ballerina."

Camilla grabbed for her towel. "I *am* a ballerina, you idiots."

"So dance for us," Debbie said. "Show us what you can do."

I knew I should do something, stop them, but part of me thrummed with desire. Part of me wanted to join in.

"—and don't go running to Mr. Principal, because he doesn't give a fuck," Anna Maria was saying. "He hates you as much as we do."

Oh god. Mr. Van Housen. The last thing I needed was to be dragged to his office again, a witness for the second time. What would Bitsy say to that?

I made myself turn away, telling myself it was none of my business. Anyway, it wasn't as if anyone was actually getting hurt. Coach Shaw would come soon to hurry everyone to their next class, and Debbie and Anna Maria would drop the game. Camilla would be fine.

I felt like throwing up.

🐈

I returned home to another of Dad's guilt offerings, this time a silver pendant from Macedonia. The pendant hung from a black silk cord, and it was in the shape of a J, for Jane. Because clearly, in Dad's mind, I was still learning my letters—or at least still wearing them around my neck, as the fad had been in elementary school.

I could wear the necklace if I wanted to, and people would see it as a kitschy-cool. Soon every girl in school would have her first initial dangling from a cord. Or, more likely, they'd all have my first initial dangling from cords. An army of glittering Js.

Only that would be way too depressing.

I lowered the pendant onto my dresser. Sometimes I didn't know which was worse: the possibility that Dad would keep sending these inane gifts, when all they did was remind me of what I didn't have, or the possibility that one day he would stop.

Out of nowhere, a memory wormed in. Me, huddled naked in an empty bathtub, because I didn't know how to work the faucets. I must have been about five, and usually Mom ran my bath for me. But that night, Dad was on duty. "You can do it," he'd said, barely looking up from his magazine. "You're a big girl."

When he'd come to check on me half an hour later, *still* huddling naked in the empty tub, his face had caved in. "Oh, baby," he'd said. "Why didn't you call me?"

Remembering, the stupid familiar ache opened up inside me. Did Dad ever feel this ache? No, I didn't think so, or he would be here. So if he didn't care, why did I?

I opened my dresser drawer and scooped the necklace toward me, letting it fall in with the other Dad dross. Then I paused. *Wait a minute, wait just a minute . . .*

Lurl.

Yes. It was perfect.

Excitement swelled inside me. No more stealing, and Alicia would be free. And hey, thanks to Dad I had tons of crap I could give away. A piece of crap a week, no problem. Even non-crap if it came down to it. I could take the loss.

I snatched back the pendant and did a happy dance on my

blue shag carpet, gyrating my hips. It lasted about a minute before I was hit with reality. Because they would have figured it out before, wouldn't they? If it were possible to beat the system, wouldn't Bitsy and Keisha and Mary Bryan all be offering up junk of their own?

Unless I was the only one smart enough to think of it. Unless they liked siphoning off other girls' popularity—which in Bitsy's case seemed almost certainly true.

Or maybe—aha—maybe they *were* putting their own lip balms and clippies on Lurl the Pearl's desk. Maybe I wasn't the only one to think of it; maybe I was just the last to think of it. And they were all cackling secretly to themselves as they waited for me to catch on. Well, hahaha, they wouldn't be laughing for long.

Then the *oh, shit* feeling descended again as I realized the flaw in my logic. If the object I offered Lurl was mine, then it would be my popularity that would be siphoned off. And bestowed upon . . . me, as the object-giver? Which would mean I'd have the same amount of popularity as I'd started with, no more and no less. Which wasn't *so* bad, really . . .

Except I wouldn't have the bonus bit from Alicia anymore. I'd return to non-Bitch status, which would totally suck.

I lay back on my bed and groaned.

"Jane?" Mom called. "Everything all right?"

I popped up. Jesus, she was right outside my door. "Everything's fine," I said. "What are you doing?"

She pushed in and sat down beside me. "Hey, baby," she said.
She pulled me into a sideways hug. Recently she'd been very
huggy. "Not to be nosy, but you've seemed kind of stressed the
last couple of days. Anything bothering you?"

I relaxed against her, soaking in her Mom-ness. She smelled
like leftover Chinese food. "Not really," I said. "Just, you know,
high school."

"Hmm. Yeah. I remember those days." She combed my hair
with her fingers. "Want to talk about it?"

"Nah."

"Okay." She held me for a little while longer, then gave me a
parting squeeze and stood up. "You're a good person, Jane. I love
you more and more each day."

I felt a pang.

"Night, doll." She pulled the door shut behind her.

I flopped back on the bed. The pendant, still in my hand, had
grown warm from my touch.

Screw it, I decided. It wasn't really mine; I'd had it for less than
a day. Tomorrow I'd give it to Lurl, and whatever would happen
would happen.

As I was brushing my teeth, it came to me that I no longer doubted
that all this was real. The offerings, the siphoning of power. Lurl.
No longer was I saying to myself, "Oh, baloney. You don't really
believe this stuff, do you?" Because I did believe, I guess ever since

that moment in geometry when the world slipped to the side. When I saw how just a shimmering shadow separated what could and couldn't be.

My toothbrush stilled as I thought again of Sandy, whose need for affirmation ran too deep. Who died for her sins. But that would never happen to me, because I wasn't like that. Maybe I used to be, but not anymore.

I brushed hard to combat the sudden sourness of my breath. When I spit, my toothpaste was tinged with blood.

"Um, no," Keisha said. She dangled the J from her slender fingers, then yanked upward on the cord, caught the pendant in her palm, and shoved the whole thing into the pocket of my denim jacket.

"Not cool," she said as I stumbled backward. "Lurl told me you put it on her desk, trying to pass it off as a proper offering. Did you honestly think she wouldn't know?"

"I just thought . . . I mean, I was only—"

Keisha waved her hand. "Don't."

I knew I was bright red, because I could feel the heat in my face. Being scolded by Keisha was horrible, worse by far than if it were Mary Bryan or even Bitsy.

Keisha walked farther away from Hamilton Hall, indicating with a head jerk that I was to follow. She stepped around a tabby cat basking in the sun. It regarded us with indolent amber eyes. When we were clearly, absolutely alone, she said, "It's been a week, Jane. You're neglecting your responsibilities."

"I know. I'm sorry. It's just . . ." I knew that nothing I could say would make it better. "I don't like that part."

She put her hands on her hips. "What part?"

My voice went even tinier. "The stealing."

The look Keisha flashed me was wounded as well as pissed, as if I'd been incredibly tacky to mention it.

"It's the way it works," she said in clipped tones. "For one to rise, another must fall."

"But *why*? Why can't we just rise, and everybody else can stay where they are? I wouldn't care!"

"And you think I would?" Keisha demanded. She glared at me, then visibly pulled herself back. When she exhaled, her nostrils flared. "Say you've taken a math test. Or an English test, since you love books so much. And you get a hundred. You're psyched, right? 'Mom, I got a hundred! I got the highest grade in the class!'" She raised her eyebrows. "But say everybody else gets a hundred, too. Are you still as proud?"

"Of course," I said stubbornly. "I'd still have my A."

"Bullshit. You like your As because other people get Cs. Because that means you're smarter than they are. Better than they are."

"I don't think I'm better than anyone."

"Then you're an idiot."

Behind us, kids ambled out of Hamilton on the way to their next class. Two girls giggled loudly from the other side of the quad.

"I'm not saying it's fair," Keisha said. "But *life* isn't fair. Some people are boring and stupid no matter how you cut it. You can try to make conversation with them all day, and they're still boring and stupid."

"So, what? They should be shot?"

"Yeah, they should be shot," she said sarcastically. "Steal a barrette, shoot them in the head—what's the difference?"

Keisha's cell phone jingled. Her eyes flew to mine.

I held out my hands, like, *Hey, it's not me calling you.*

She dug for her phone. Turning her body from mine, she muttered, "This better be important. I'm at school."

I walked a couple of feet away and feigned interest in the giggling girls on the quad. By the sound of it, they were pretending to be dinosaurs. "Aaaah-roooo!" one bellowed, dipping her voice way down and then raising it up into her higher register. "Aaaah-*roooo!*"

"No," Keisha said. "I told you, six o'clock."

"Mmmm-waaaah!" the other dinosaur girl responded.

Keisha hunched her shoulders and put her hand up to her ear. "Call your sponsor," she said, raising her voice over the noise. "Call your *sponsor.*" She paced in a tight circle. "Fine, I'll be there. I said I would, all right? I have to go, Mom. I've got class."

She hit the end button.

"Mmraah-wah-*oooo!*" trumpeted girl number one.

Keisha scowled. "What the hell are they doing?"

"I have no idea. Pretending to be dinosaurs?"

Her scowl deepened. She looked at me, and she didn't have to say it.

"Maybe it's for a play," I said feebly.

Keisha strode back toward Hamilton. "You're one of the lucky ones, Jane. Don't blow it."

I hurried to catch up with her. "Just one quick thing."

She didn't stop. "What?"

"Why did you really pick me? The truth."

Now she stopped. She turned around. "Because you were broken. Just like us."

Bitsy snuck up on me in the library, where I'd gone to muddle things out. Because what did Keisha mean, "broken"? My thoughts flitted again to Sandy's neediness—was that the kind of "broken" she meant? But in my case Keisha had spoken in past tense, as in I used to be broken but now was fixed. I thought of that gospel song Mom sang when she did laundry: *I once was lost, but now am found. Was blind but now I see.*

"Amazing Grace."

Was that how it was for me?

"Boo," Bitsy said.

I jumped.

"Ha," she said. "Gotcha." She came around the back of my chair and lounged against the work surface of the carrel. Her Powerpuff Girls shirt hugged her body.

"What's up?" I said, trying my best to act cool. "Have you come to yell at me?"

"Pardon?"

I swallowed. This was the first time I'd seen Bitsy since Anna Maria and Debbie had tormented Camilla during PE, and it made me feel weird. I kind of wanted to talk to Bitsy about it, but at the same time I kind of really didn't.

"Keisha got all mad at me about the Lurl thing," I said. "She was like, 'You're neglecting your responsibilities. You're letting us down.'"

"And right she is," Bitsy said. "Trying to pass off your own necklace as someone else's, you poor sod. Think no one's tried that one before?"

I looked at her from under my bangs.

"Bet you about wet your pants putting it on Lurl's desk, too. And now you have to do it all over again. Life's a bitch, eh?"

Was she teasing me? I got the strangest feeling she was teasing me.

"I don't want everyone to hate me," I said. "I didn't mean to let you guys down."

"I know, luv," Bitsy said. "And that's why I've decided to help you out." She fished into the pocket of her jeans. She drew out a brown bobby pin. "Here."

I looked at Bitsy, then back at the bobby pin.

"Don't go getting used to it," Bitsy said. "I'm not going to bail you out every time."

I gazed at the bobby pin's brown ridges. Finally I said, "But . . . I'm not the one who took it."

Bitsy tilted her hand, and the bobby pin dropped to the floor. She lifted her eyebrows.

"Whose is it?" I asked.

"No one's. Not your darling Alicia's, if that's what you're worried about."

Still, I hesitated.

"Fine. If you don't want it—"

"No, I do," I said. I bent to retrieve it, my face at Bitsy's shoes. Strappy black sandals, even though fall was officially upon us. A silver ring on her second toe.

"Brilliant," Bitsy said. "Lurl will be so pleased."

On the way to Lurl's office, I spotted Alicia trailing out of her geometry class. The other kids strolled out in groups of two or three, chatting and laughing, and then there was Alicia, all alone. I knew in my gut that I should go talk to her, but I didn't want to. *Not the right time,* I told myself.

Except that unfortunately, she'd spotted me, too. "Jane!" she called.

I walked faster, eyes straight ahead, then gave up when she touched my shoulder.

"Jane," she said. "Jesus, are you deaf?"

I turned around, trying to tell myself that the yuck factor I felt didn't have to do with her. I was in a hurry and she was interrupting me, that's all.

"Alicia!" I said. "Hi! So how'd it go Saturday night? With Tommy. Oh my god, I've been dying to hear."

Alicia narrowed her eyes, her black hair lanky around her face. "Yeah, which is why you've been avoiding me all week."

"I haven't been avoiding you. Why would you even say that?"

"Uh, because it's true?"

My smile cracked. If I were in Alicia's shoes, I would at least try to be nice. "So are you going to tell me about Tommy or not?"

"He canceled," Alicia said. "An hour before he was supposed to pick me up."

What cheerfulness I'd mustered crumbled to dust. It was like a lead weight dropping down inside me, and not only because I was sad for Alicia—if I even was sad for Alicia. It was more the tiredness of realizing, *Oh shit, now I have to deal with this on top of everything else.*

"That sucks. What a jerk."

"He said he'd gotten the date wrong. He was like, 'But let's do something another time, okay?'"

"Oh, well that's different."

"How? He totally blew me off."

"He didn't blow you off. He just, you know, rescheduled."

She made an extremely irritating face. "Do you have any idea how fake you sound? I'm serious. Do you?"

I gritted my teeth. If she wanted to be this way, fine. It wasn't my job to coddle her. "Look," I said. "I'm trying to be supportive, but it's hard when you're so nasty all the time. You ever think maybe that's why Tommy canceled?"

She flinched. Like she was honestly surprised, when here she was acting like a grade-A prat, as Bitsy would say.

Then her eyes went small. "Screw you," she said.

"Screw me?" I said. "Screw you! All I've done is try to help!"

She poked my chest. "Rae was right. You've lost your soul."

Anger flamed through me—anger and fear and other things, too. But instead of retaliating, I stuffed it down and walked away.

Keisha was right. Some people *were* boring and stupid no matter how you cut it.

Still, I couldn't quite catch my breath. I almost wanted to go back and shove her, spill her backpack again so I could snatch a pen. Or another tub of her pointless lip balm, because who would ever want to kiss those lying lips? No one, that's who.

She was the toad. Not me.

I put the bobby pin on Lurl's desk, closing my mind to whom it might have once belonged. It was easier than I thought. And an hour later, as I gathered my books from my locker, I felt the spine-tingling surge that meant Lurl had claimed the offering. It filled me up and left me breathless.

That evening, after an impromptu *Through the Looking Glass* theme party at Sukie Karing's house, I played back a sad-sack message from Alicia.

"Um, hi, it's me," she said in a snivelly voice. "I hope you're not mad at me. I know I was really rude, but I didn't mean to be. It's just, what you said, it really . . ." She sniffed. "Anyway, I'm sorry. That's all I wanted to say."

The first message was followed by a second. This time I could hear Rae in the background.

"Um, hi again," Alicia said.

Then Rae: "Tell her, Alicia. Just say the words on the paper."

"I can't!"

"*Say* it!"

Alicia came back full strength, as if she'd removed her hand from the part you speak into. "Um, sorry, Jane. That was just Rae. Anyway—"

"She hates your guts! She thinks you're scum!"

"No, I don't! Oh my god, *Rae*! Jane, I swear—"

Her voice cut off, and the machine beeped, announcing the third and last message.

"This is Rae. My sister hates your guts, even if she's too afraid to admit it. And I do, too. Everyone does. They may not act like it on the surface, but we all know that what's on the surface is a big, fat lie. So take that and shove it up your bunghole, you lying bitch!"

Three final beeps, then silence, except for the ticking of the oven clock.

"Psychotic freak," I whispered.

My legs felt shaky. I hit "delete."

Saturday night was casino night at Stuart Hill's house. Stuart's probation was over, and to celebrate, his parents had hired a croupier to run a blackjack table in their living room. A roulette wheel clicked and whirred in the alcove, and in the oversized den, three showgirls danced in Cleopatra headdresses and black sequined fantails.

Bitsy smooched with Ryan Overturf by the slot machine in the entry hall, then tired of his fawning and called for a Bitches meeting away from any nosy parkers. I was reluctant to leave the bar, where Nate had been showing me the impossibility of burning a cigarette hole on a twenty dollar bill laid flat against his arm. Apparently the flesh behind the bill took the heat, and sure enough, when Nate removed the bill, I could see a small red blister rising on his skin. I would have kissed it to make it better, but duty called. I trailed the others out to the patio.

"It's ten o'clock, and already I'm knackered," Bitsy complained.

"What about your new flame Ryan?" Mary Bryan asked. "You seemed happy enough five minutes ago."

"Five minutes ago he hadn't yet confessed his undying love for me," Bitsy said. "'Be still my heart'—he actually said those very words! Swooning about like an idiot, saying it was a dream come true. Bloody nightmare, I say!"

"You don't want to be his dream come true?" I asked.

Bitsy rolled her eyes. She was gorgeous even when she was fed up, and in her low-cut red dress, she was every guy's dream come true. "It was a *kiss*. A simple, ordinary kiss. I swear, I thought he was going to break out in song."

"Then why'd you come on to him?" Keisha said. Tonight her dress was teal. It shimmered as she took a sip of her Diet Coke. "You knew what would happen."

"Bloody hell," Bitsy said. "Pammy can have him. They can slobber all over each other and leave me out of it." She pulled a compact from her tiny red clutch and checked her makeup. She uncapped a lipstick and applied a fresh coat. "He asked me to go to the Fall Fling with him, can you believe it?" She dropped the lipstick back in her bag. "I told him sorry, but we girls are going together."

"We are?" Mary Bryan said.

"Fine with me," Keisha said. "L'Kardos has an away meet that weekend, anyway."

Mary Bryan shrugged. She was dressed as a flapper, her hair swooped back in adorable pin-curl waves. "I guess it's okay with me, too."

They looked at me expectantly.

"Jane?" Bitsy inquired.

I smoothed my new skirt, which I'd bought with Mom's credit card. "The thing is, I kind of already have a date. With Phil Fleischman?"

"Phil *Fleischman*?" Mary Bryan said.

"What?" I said. "What's wrong with Phil?"

Bitsy smothered a laugh. "Oh, sweets. Phil may be a nice lad, but come on. He's puny."

My cheeks burned. "Puny" was a terrible word.

"Come with us," Mary Bryan said. "Phil will understand."

Bitsy looped her arm through mine. "Girl power and all that. Tell him it's a unity thing."

Keisha watched my face. "You don't have to, Jane."

"Yes, you do," Bitsy said. "Otherwise there'd just be the three of us, and how sad would that be?"

I bit my lip. I imagined being at the Fall Fling with Phil, watching as Keisha, Bitsy, and Mary Bryan frolicked about without me. Then I imagined it the other way around, with Phil watching from the sidelines. Only he probably wouldn't come on his own. It's not as if he really liked school functions, anyway.

"I guess I could do something with Phil another night," I said. I was just trying out the idea, but Bitsy squeezed my arm approvingly.

"That's our girl," she said. She sat down on a wicker bench and patted the cushions to show that we should join her. "And now for more pressing concerns. What in heaven's name shall we wear?"

On our way back through the house, we were waylaid by Elizabeth Greene and several of the other cheerleaders. They were perched on one of the living room sofas, cackling at something on somebody's laptop.

"Check it out," Elizabeth said, grabbing Bitsy's arm. She pulled Bitsy over and pointed midway down the screen. "Look what we put for 'favorite movie.'"

"*Bad Girls' Dormitory,*" Bitsy read. Her lips curved into a smile. "Is that the one with Alyssa Milano?"

"And for favorite Web rings, we put 'Naughty Professors,' 'Prince Edward's Lesbigay Social Club,' and 'Asian Sluts.'"

"Brilliant. Only she's not Asian," Bitsy pointed out.

"What, she's not allowed to have a fetish?" Elizabeth said.

"Who's not allowed to have a fetish?" Mary Bryan asked. She squeezed past me to get closer to the computer.

Until now, I'd only been half paying attention. Keisha had spotted L'Kardos slipping a bill into the bra of one of the show-girls, and she'd marched over to slap his hand. Seeing him had made me think of Nate, and I'd been scanning the dimly lit room for his lean frame.

But then Elizabeth said, "Camilla Jones," and the back of my neck prickled. At least, I thought she said "Camilla Jones." Did she say "Camilla Jones"?

I shook my head to clear it. "I'm sorry. Who'd you say you're talking about?"

"For favorite music, how about this," Elizabeth said. "Up with People, Backstreet Boys, and the Sex Pistols."

"What about that guy who plays the pan flute?" Mary Bryan suggested.

Elizabeth giggled. She typed in, "And that guy who plays the pan flute."

"I'm totally lost," I said.

"It's a 'Friendies' profile," Elizabeth said proudly. She scrolled to the top, where sure enough, there was Camilla's name, along with her measurements, her favorite food, and her favorite color. For that one, Elizabeth had entered, "The rainbow."

"You know, a hook-up club," Elizabeth explained. "We gave out her home phone, too. And her street address. Want to see the photo we submitted?"

She clicked on another link, and up came the picture. Camilla's hair was pulled back into a severe bun, and her lips were pursed. Offering contrast to Camilla's scowl was a flock of doting bluebirds, which Elizabeth had pasted in so that they appeared to be sitting on Camilla's shoulders.

I battled with my natural impulse, which was to laugh. Only in reality it *wasn't* my natural impulse, and I knew it. My breathing grew shallow.

"I took it on my camera-phone yesterday during lunch," Jerri Skyler volunteered. "First I made Clark throw a cherry tomato at her."

"But why?" I said.

"To make her look up," Jerri said.

"No, I mean why are you doing this in the first place? What if some weirdo actually tracks her down?"

Elizabeth winked. "Then maybe she'll make a friend."

"A friendie," Jerri corrected.

They all cracked up. I didn't want to be there, so I left. Bitsy followed me into the hall.

"Chill," she said. "It was my idea. I thought it would be good for a laugh."

I wrapped my arms around my chest. I was a bad person, but at least I tried to rein myself in. And I knew I was indebted to Bitsy, but why did she always have to make things harder?

"I don't get it," I said. "You're, like, the most adored girl in the school. You've got everything you want. Why do you have to make everyone be mean to her?"

Bitsy wagged her finger. "You've got to admit, Camilla is very antisocial. It's not healthy."

It pissed me off that she was being so flippant. The whole situation pissed me off, my own reaction included. "And this is your way of bringing her out of her shell? Signing her up for an online stalker service?"

"She's a stuck-up cunt. If she didn't think she was so much better than us, none of this would be happening."

"Oh, that's nice," I said. My anger flared higher. It was her fault I felt so ragged inside. So I said, "Why do you even care what Camilla does? Seriously, does it bug you that much that she knows about your dad?"

Her face went slack. Then her eyes flashed poison and she said, "What did you say?"

I realized I'd screwed up, but it was too late to recant. "Nothing! Just that . . ." I threw up my hands. "Dads leave. That's what they do."

She lifted her chin. "And of course you know all about it, being the resident expert. How long's yours been gone, two years now?"

"Three," I threw back. "But you don't see me ruining people's lives just for the fun of it."

"Oh, so you did your friend Alicia a favor, then, did you?"

"I didn't know what I was doing. I didn't—"

"Face it, Jane. You're no better than I am."

"Maybe not. But at least I want to be."

She stepped closer. For a second I thought she was going to— what? Slap me? Then a movement at the end of the hall drew her attention. It was Mary Bryan, wandering out of the living room.

"*There* you guys are," she said. She glanced from me to Bitsy. "What? What's going on?"

"Jane's been prattling on about how virtuous she is because she feels sorry for poor Camilla," Bitsy said.

Mary Bryan wrinkled her forehead. "Camilla? Why?" Then, as if it honestly that second occurred to her, "Oh. Because of the 'Friendies' thing?"

"And you need to keep your blabbing mouth shut," Bitsy added, making Mary Bryan flinch. Bitsy spun on her heel and strode down the hall. Halfway to the front door, she turned around.

"By the way, it was her bobby pin," she said, way too casually. "But you already knew that, didn't you? Look deep into your saintly heart and tell me you didn't know."

Bitsy left, leaving me and Mary Bryan alone in the hall. After a moment, Mary Bryan looked at me.

"Thanks a fucking lot," she said. "There goes our ride."

After Stuart's party, things weren't the same between me and the others. Still, I kept my word and canceled my date with Phil so that we could go to the Fall Fling as a holly jolly foursome. Because what was I going to do, walk away from the Bitches in protest of Bitsy's fucked-up-ness? Let them reap all the glory while I glowered from the sidelines? They were stuck with me, and I was stuck with them. I wasn't about to give up what I'd worked so hard to earn.

"Tell me you're kidding," Phil had said when I called him. "Please tell me you're not ditching me to be with them."

"I'm *not*," I said. "It's just, you know, a girl thing. A ladies' night out."

"In other words, you're ditching me to be with them."

My fingers tightened around the phone.

"Janie, come on," he said in a wheedling voice that made him seem spineless. "This is me."

"Yeah, and you hate school functions. That's what you've always said, that you can't even stand going to them and—"

"Fine," he said. "Forget it." The wheedling was gone, replaced by a stiffness that cut right through me. "But I never would have done this to you, Jane. And you know it."

My heart felt bruised. "Okay," I whispered.

He hung up.

Keisha, Mary Bryan, and Bitsy all tried to shake some sense into me. They each did it separately, as if they didn't want the others to know. It would have been funny under different circumstances. Instead it was just pathetic.

Mary Bryan approached me on Monday afternoon. She tracked me down in the farthest back library carrel, where I'd retreated after our lunchtime schmooze-fest with the girls' soccer team.

"Oh, *Ramona the Brave*!" she exclaimed, nudging down the spine of my paperback so she could see the title. "I loved that book when I was little!"

I regarded her from under my bangs. I'd done my bit in the cafeteria, playing to our audience as was expected. But one-on-one, I'd resolved to play it cool. It was hard, though, because just being near her made those waves of liking swell back up again.

"That's the one where those boys call Beezus 'Jesus Beezus,' right?" Mary Bryan said. "And Ramona gets all tough and tells them off?" She put her fists on her hips and scowled a six-year-old's scowl. "'*Do not take the Lord's name in vain!*'"

"What do you want, Mary Bryan?"

She dropped the cutesy act. She pulled up a chair, its front leg knocking against the edge of the carrel. "Why are you mad at me? That 'Friendies' thing was Bitsy's deal, not mine."

"You thought it was hilarious."

"So? It's not hurting anybody."

"It isn't?"

She fiddled with her bracelet. It was silver, a chain of tiny flowers. She let it go and changed tactics. "You know, it kind of pissed me off what you said about Bitsy's dad after swearing you wouldn't. I called Bitsy the next day. She told me everything that happened."

My stomach tightened despite myself. "I didn't mean to. It just came out."

"Well. Just so you know."

The library was empty except for the two of us and Ms. Cratchett, who was trying to get one of the feral cats off her desk. The cat lay draped over the top of the computer, and Ms. Cratchett's "scats" were having no effect. If she were a good librarian, she'd forget the cat and scold us instead.

"Look," Mary Bryan said. "You're not going to do anything stupid, are you?"

"What are you talking about?"

"We all go through it, the whole 'Is it right?' thing. But that's why we picked you, Jane. You're, like, a force for the good."

"Mary Bryan, I don't know what you're talking about."

She looked annoyed, as if she wanted to call me on it. But I was telling the truth. I *didn't* know what she was talking about.

"Keisha's careful about who she picks," she said. "And so am I."

"To steal from, you mean?"

Mary Bryan's eyes flew to Ms. Cratchett, who was now nudging the cat's haunches in a series of tentative jabs. The cat regarded her with lids at half mast.

"Shhh," Mary Bryan said.

"She's not paying attention," I said. I waved my hands, went "la, la, la" in a medium-loud voice. "See?"

Ms. Cratchett looked up. Her expression was frazzled and a little wild. "Girls. Keep it down."

I blushed. The cat swished its tail.

In a whisper, Mary Bryan said, "The three of us can band together, you and me and Keisha. We'll tell Bitsy that she *has* to rotate around. And that she has to pick people who are already popular, like we do, so that it doesn't matter so much. It's only fair."

My stomach went rock hard, because I suddenly knew where she was heading. And I didn't want to hear it.

"I know," Mary Bryan said, reading my face. "It's terrible. Because with Camilla, it's like she doesn't even have any popularity left to be taken. At this point it's probably more like anti-popularity. Going deep into the negatives, or something like that." She squeezed my knee. "That's why it's so important that you're on our side."

Something foul rose in my throat. I'd seen what taking Alicia's lip balm had done to Alicia—and that was just one time, with Alicia being allowed to bounce back after the fact. At least, hypothetically, although I'd yet to see much improvement. But Camilla was never allowed to bounce back, because Bitsy stole from her every single week. That's what Mary Bryan was talking about. Sometimes she even enlisted assistants.

"Jane, are you okay?" Mary Bryan asked.

"I need to go. I need to go to the bathroom."

"Oh. Oh! Okay, sure." She slid back her chair. "So . . . you're not going to bail on us?"

I stumbled past her, noting as if from far away her look of concern.

"Jane?"

I pushed down my nausea as best I could and told the truth. "God, Mary Bryan. It hadn't even crossed my mind."

Keisha's appeal came as an e-mail:

Jane,

I know you're going through a hard time right now. You're questioning all sorts of stuff, and maybe you're even wondering what's right and what's wrong. That's okay. It just means you're a good person.

But there's something you should know. The other girls need us—and I'm not talking about Bitsy and Mary Bryan. I'm talking about everyone else. Even your friend Alicia. Even Camilla.

We're their royalty. We make their lives special.

I know it's hard sometimes, but that's why we have each other.

Keisha

I rested my forehead on the base of my palm and closed my eyes.

The whole thing made me so tired.

I lifted my head and typed in, "Got your message. Thanks." I hit the send button, then deleted her name from my inbox.

Out of all three, Bitsy was the most straightforward. She must have sweet-talked one of the administrative assistants into giving her my combination, because on Tuesday I found a black VHS tape in my locker. It was unlabeled, but I knew what it was.

I didn't plan on watching it. I was going to throw it away unviewed. But when I got home, I pulled it from my backpack and turned it over in my hands. It looked harmless, like the cassette on top of our television labeled "Jane's Tacky TV Tape," on which I recorded episodes of *The Gilmore Girls* and *Survivor: Senior High.*

I knew the tape from Bitsy wasn't harmless. But some fatalistic part of me made me walk across the room and pop it into the VCR. Maybe it's not as bad as I think, I reasoned.

There was Kyle's living room, just as I remembered it. There was Sukie Karing, laughing with Pammy Varlotta. And there was me, horrible in that peasant blouse that definitely *was* too see-through, despite Mary Bryan's assurances. Heat pricked my scalp as I watched myself edge up to group after group of glossy partiers, only to slink away like a scolded puppy.

"Yo, dude," Stuart said at one point, catching me on film after swinging away from a shot of Bitsy and Brad. "Check out Freaky Freshman. Where you going now, Freaky Freshman?"

Freaky Freshman—that was me—was sneaking into Kyle's kitchen. Glancing around, then darting past the counter. Ducking behind the island. Gone.

"Holy shit, she's *hiding*!" Stuart crowed. "I gotta tell Bitsy!"
I punched the off button, shame washing over me in scalding waves. Punched the button again to eject the cassette, then yanked it from the VCR and dug at the shiny tape. It spun loose and pooled in my lap.

She'd known I was there. She'd known I was there and had never said a word.

I ripped at the tape, but it wouldn't tear. It only stretched and ruffled at the edges.

"Dammit," I cried.

"Jane?" Mom said. "What's going on?"

My eyes flew to Mom, who stood in the doorframe with a

chubby manilla envelope in her hand. My heart beat crazily in my chest.

"Wild guess. VCR troubles?"

I lowered my hands, still twined with tape. I tried to clump the whole jumble into a pile.

"It's been a little temperamental," she said. "One of these days I'll take it to a fix-it guy." She came in the room, put down the package, and squatted beside me. "Here, let me help."

"No!" I said. "I mean, no, that's okay. It's my mess. I'll clean it up."

She looked at me. "Are you all right, sweetie?"

"Huh? Yeah, I'm great. I'm super."

"Are you sure?"

"Yes, I'm sure." I laughed. "Mom. Quit staring at me."

Mom put her hand on my cheek, cupping it. "I love you so much, Jane. Sometimes it feels overwhelming, did you know that?"

"Gee, Mom. Thanks for sharing."

Her shoulders dropped, and I felt guilty. Then she groaned and creaked to her feet. "Oh, I'm getting old."

"No, you're not."

She gestured at the package on the coffee table. "That's from your dad. From an island in the South Pacific."

I sank further within myself. "Terrific. Maybe it's a VCR repair kit."

A ghost of a smile graced her face. "Guess I better put together some dinner. I'll call you when it's ready."

When she was gone, I gathered up the wrecked cassette and carted it out to the big green garbage can in our garage. I shoved it under a plastic shopping bag and a stray egg carton. I dumped some potting soil on top for good measure, then banged shut the lid.

Back inside, I opened Dad's gift. It was a Polynesian vest made of quilted cotton, with cheerful yellow sunshines stitched across the chest.

On a card was a scrawled message. "Saw this and thought of you," it said. "Hugs and kisses, Dad."

Thursday morning Sukie Karing showed up wearing jeans like mine and a T-shirt identical to the one I'd worn the day before. It was white with red ribbing around the neck and sleeves, and on the upper left corner it read THE ADVERTISEMENT IS ON THE BACK. The back showed a cartoon gunslinger twirling two guns. Above him, a banner read DIRTY DAN'S SALOON.

"I had it specially made," Sukie confided. "We're like twins, even though you're not wearing yours today. Maybe next week we can coordinate!"

I should have been flattered—and okay, I was—but I felt weird, too. Sukie could play twinsies with me, and her stock would go up. But if Camilla wore that shirt, would everyone think *she* was adorable? No.

But Sukie was Sukie, not Camilla. Sukie wasn't a Bitch, but as I'd told Phil, she had her own little cache of popularity. That's what I reminded myself when, as I returned her hug, I slipped my hand into her purse, which hung open and inviting from her shoulder. Because Bitsy's tape had worked: there was no way in hell I was going back to the pre-Bitch me.

Better Sukie than someone else, I told myself. That and, *It's only for a week.*

Sukie released me, pink with pleasure. And although her hand strayed to her purse, fumbling for the clasp and hiking the strap higher on her shoulder, she didn't realize anything was missing.

"I am just so happy," she bubbled. "My life is so great. I mean, not like yours, obviously, but I don't even care—that's how happy I am!" She widened her eyes. "And Fall Fling is only two days away. Aren't you just so excited you could burst?"

"I'm managing to hold it together," I said. My fingers curled around my plunder. A stick of gum? A little on the linty side from the feel of it.

The warning bell rang, and Sukie made a face. "Trig," she said. "Yuckers."

I nodded sympathetically.

"But we're on for lunch, right?" She squeezed my arm. "I've been counting down the days. Bye!"

I waited until she was officially gone, then unfurled my fingers.

Juicy Fruit, my favorite.

On my way to Lurl's office, I passed a man wearing elbow-length leather gloves and a work shirt that said ANIMAL CONTROL. He was scowling at the ceiling, his hands on his hips.

I stopped. I watched him for a couple of seconds. "What are you doing?" I finally asked.

"Those damn cats," he grunted. "They've taken over the duct-work."

I glanced up at the rectangular ceiling tiles, smooth and white with little dots on them. I got a jittery feeling of wanting to laugh.

"So, what, you're telling me they're up there above us?" I joked. "Running wild through the ceiling?"

His scowl deepened, and I followed his gaze in time to see one of the ceiling tiles shift a fraction of an inch. We heard a skittering, followed by a meow. A crumble of cardboardy stuff landed on the man's shirt.

"That answer your question?" the man said.

My smile fell away. I thought of paws padding through dark spaces, and a chill moved through me.

"Well . . . good luck," I said. I realized I actually meant it. "I hope you catch them."

I walked quickly down the hall, through the heavy door, and into the connecting corridor. I unlocked Lurl's office and slipped inside. I expected the room to be empty, as it had always been before, so I about crapped my pants when I heard her deep voice.

"Lookie, lookie, who's got the cookie," she chortled from behind her desk. She held out her hand. "Gimme."

The smell of cat food was stronger than ever, but there was still no sign of where it came from. Just her bare office, sterile and gray. The door at the far end leading to . . . wherever it led. *Perhaps to an empty storage room?* I shooed the thought from my head.

I dug into my pocket and pulled out Sukie's gum. I hesitated, then stepped forward and placed it in Lurl's palm. I didn't look at the pencil sharpener.

"What will you do with it?" I asked.

She ran the gum under her nose. She sniffed. "Smelly papers—that's what we used to call the wrappers. I collected them, you know. In a box under my bed."

I swallowed.

She tapped the gum against her desk. "What will I do with it? What I always do, of course." She giggled her man giggle. "Curiosity killed the cat, you know."

My heart crawled up my throat. I couldn't have spoken if I'd wanted to.

She stopped smiling, and the tip of her tongue snaked out in disapproval. I got the sense that my reaction didn't please her.

"I was crowned the Ice Maiden," she said in a scolding voice.

"What?" I croaked.

"Of the Winter Carnival. I wore all white."

She's shy, Mary Bryan had said. *Shy my ass.*

"That's great," I said. "I bet you looked great." I edged toward the door, but a crazy braveness made me ask one last thing. "I hope this doesn't come out the wrong way, but . . . why do they call you Lurl the Pearl?"

She leaned forward, and her T strap glinted in the dim light. "Because I'm such a gem."

When the jolt came, it blissed me out. I gave myself over to it and wished it lasted longer.

The theme for the Fall Fling was "Neverland," which cracked me up, because without meaning to, the planning committee had nailed it on the head. Instead of a dance, it was a party for kids who never wanted to grow up. Who wanted to stay in high school forever.

Recently, three and a half more years of high school had started seeming like a really long time.

But, whatever. The committee had pulled out all the stops and turned the gym into a oversized playground. If I wanted to, I could get strapped into a harness and climb a rock-climbing wall, and when I got to the top I could ring a bell. Or I could get into a harness attached to a bungee cord, and a friend could, too, and we could race each other down a puffy rubber tunnel until one of us got snapped back by the force of the bungee. Or I could get strapped into a giant transparent bowling ball, and two of the chaperones would roll me down a lane set up with oversized bowling pins.

"Dude," Ryan Overturf said, slapping Nate Solomon's hand. He laughed at how funny it was, all these grown-ups going to so much trouble. "This rules."

"Yeah, baby," Nate said, glancing at me to make sure I heard. I smiled at him, and my heart gave a happy, nervous jump. Despite the weirdness of everything else, my crush on Nate still thrilled me. He'd been showing off for me ever since we got here. I knew it because I could feel it.

"Yo," Ryan said. He jerked his chin at an inflated rubber dome that was supposed to be a boxing ring. You could put on big ol' helmets and big ol' boxing gloves—like, the size of pillows—and go at it with your buddies. Ryan stepped closer to Bitsy and threw his arm around her shoulders. "You and me, Bits. I want to rough you up, sweet cakes."

"Why are they here?" Mary Bryan said in a low voice. She tugged at her gold halter. "I thought this was a girls' night. I thought that was the plan."

"Don't get your knickers in a bunch," Bitsy whispered in return. She removed Ryan's arm. "You go on, boys. Show us how it's done."

Ryan's chest puffed out. "Come on, dickhead," he said to Nate. "You heard the ladies."

When they were gone, Keisha bumped me with her hip. "Looks like you've got an admirer," she said. "Nate couldn't take his eyes off you."

At the mention of his name, a warmth spread through me. "Please," I said.

"You know it's true," Mary Bryan teased. "You're a princess, and he wants to be your prince."

"My *prince*?"

Her lips twitched, and I knew she wasn't buying my protests. "He's yours if you want him. That's all I'm saying." She fingered the strap of my sparkly tank top. "Fabulous Jane in her fabulous new outfit. Who wouldn't want to be yours?"

They were buttering me up, I could tell. Bathing me in Bitchdom. I tried to maintain some clarity.

"Uh-huh," I said. "Only they're the totally wrong clothes for actually doing anything in."

"Which, of course, is tragic," Bitsy said. She herself was wearing a flippy black dress paired with high-heeled, knee-length black boots. "Did you *want* to slip on the Velcro suit and fling yourself at a wall?"

"The human fly," Mary Bryan intoned.

We all glanced at the far end of the gym, where a spread-eagled Elizabeth Greene struggled to free herself from the Velcro-draped wall.

"Good god," Bitsy said. "Someone should put her out of her misery."

"It's better than doing nothing," I said. "I feel lame just standing here."

"Then go," Bitsy said. She fanned her hand out at the different activities. "Knock yourself out."

Our eyes met.

"Fine, I will," I said.

"Terrif," Bitsy said.

I strolled to the bungee cord race, which did look like fun in a ridiculous sort of way. I looked on as a chaperone told the guy at the front of the line to remove all of his piercings before getting into the harness.

"Even my nose ring?" the guy asked.

"Even your nose ring."

"Even my tongue ring?" The guy stuck out his tongue and waggled it back and forth.

"Your tongue ring can stay. Just keep it in your mouth."

I skimmed the rest of the line. There was Raven Holtzclaw-Fontaine in a form-fitting sleeveless dress. She shook her head, saying no to the bungee cord, but the guy she was with stepped up to get strapped in. And there was Sukie Karing, biting her cuticles. She'd slopped red punch down the front of her white top, and the girls behind her pointed and smirked. Even Pammy, who seemed to be Sukie's date, looked as if she'd rather be elsewhere.

Move on, I told myself. *No point worrying about Sukie now.*

My eyes strayed to a guy in a white leisure suit. It was a suit that could have gone either way, super dorky or super cool in a retro seventies kind of style. I saw the guy's face, and my muscles tightened. It was Phil, and I was pretty sure people weren't looking at him and thinking super cool.

My face burned, and I knew I should leave before he saw me. But first I craned my neck to see who he was with.

Standing beside him, her arm looped through his, was Oz

Spencer, wearing a hot pink dress that matched her hot pink hair. I wondered, with a surprising stab of jealousy, if she were wearing a hot pink thong.

Oz laughed and nudged Phil's shoulder, then reached up and started removing the gazillion silver earrings that studded her ears. She was going to go for it. She was going to do the bungee race with Phil.

Phil shrugged out of his jacket. As he did, he caught sight of me. His face got still.

I lifted my hand in a tentative wave. I smiled, like, *Way to go, you big stud!*

He turned his back and reached to help Oz.

I strode to the bleachers, my heart twisting. Anna Maria and Debbie from my PE class lounged on the seats.

"Jane, hey!" Anna Maria called. She beckoned me over. "What'd I tell you, huh? Does this rock or what?"

I took a seat. I smelled Peach Schnapps.

"We've already done the Human Fly and the Box Your Brains Out. Me and Little Debs *rocked*. Didn't we, Debs?" She slugged Debbie's arm. "Bam! Knock out, baby!"

"And these two sophomores behind us?" Debbie said. "They were all, 'Ooo, no! It's too scary! We'd mess up our hair!'"

"Me and Little Debs were like, 'What'd you think this was, the prom?'" Anna Maria slapped Debbie's palm.

"What about you?" Debbie asked. "You maintaining the tangible?"

"Huh?" I said.

Anna Maria cracked up. She told Debbie, "You are such a dork." To me, she said, "It's her new way of saying 'keeping it real.' Maintaining the tangible, get it?"

"Ohhh," I said. "Gotcha."

Anna Maria's laughter kept coming. "Total dorkitude maximus—that's my Debs." She reached inside her jean jacket and pulled out a flask. A cool flask, actually. Silver with delicate etchings, curved to fit against her body. She unscrewed the top and took a swig. "Want some?"

"No, thanks," I said.

"Suit yourself. Here, Little Debs." She handed over the flask. "So. After party at Bitsy's, right? Should be a rocking good time."

She and Debbie leaned against each other and snickered.

"Down with the skank," Anna Maria said.

Debbie lifted the flask. "The skank must die!"

I wasn't following. But then, they were drunk. Got the part about Bitsy's house, though. It made my stomach curl, because no one had told me about an after party.

I grabbed the flask and downed a long gulp.

"Go, baby!" Anna Maria said. "Now we're talking!"

Passing it back, I said, "I'm out of here. Got to maintain the tangible."

More cackling from the peanut gallery. "You do that," Anna Maria called. "We'll see your ass at Bitsy's!"

"Game's up, Bitsy," I said. I sounded whiny, which pissed me off. "Thanks, you know, for including me."

"What's that?" Bitsy said. She turned her attention from Bounce-a-Rama, where Stuart Hill was doing moon jumps off a glittering gray launch pad.

"Your after party. Anna Maria and Debbie told me."

Mary Bryan blushed; Bitsy didn't. Keisha dropped her eyes.

"We just . . ." Mary Bryan started. "I mean, it wasn't like we didn't want you to come, it's just—"

"Of course we want you to come," Bitsy said. "We didn't think *you'd* want to, that's all."

"Why would you think that?" I said. "Seriously. You at least could have asked me."

"You're absolutely right, and I feel like a prize idiot for being so thoughtless. But it's all out now, yeah?"

I couldn't stop fooling with my ring, using my thumb to rotate it around and around my finger. "Were you just going to drop me off and go without me? Wouldn't that make *you* feel pathetic?"

Bitsy's eyes widened. "Sweetie!" she said, as if she were truly shocked and worried. "How could you ever feel pathetic? Don't you know how much we love you?"

"We thought you were mad at us," Mary Bryan said. She kind of petted me. "I'm so glad you're not."

I couldn't let it go. I didn't know what Bitsy was up to.

"Keisha?" I said. "Do you want me to come?"

Keisha looked at me, sadly almost. Embarrassment coursed through me for being such a baby.

"I want you to do what you want to do," she said. "It's up to you."

"Well, I want to go," I said.

"Superb," Bitsy said. She turned back to the Bounce-a-Rama, where Stuart had gotten snarled in the harness. "We'll leave in a jiff."

I looked past the Bounce-a-Rama to the giant bowling ball, where I could see Phil and Oz at the front of the line. Phil said something, and Oz stuck out her tongue. A chaperone strapped her into the transparent ball, and she rolled down the puffy rubber lane, laughing like mad as her dress tangled around her legs. She careened into the bowling pins with an echoing crash.

We didn't go straight to Bitsy's. Instead, we stopped at a house five down from hers, a red brick Tudor with two stone eagles perched at the foot of the winding drive. Anna Maria and Debbie parked behind us on the street. A Jeep full of cheerleaders pulled up last.

"What's going on?" I asked from Bitsy's backseat.

"Pit stop," Bitsy said. She killed the motor and got out of the car. Keisha and Mary Bryan climbed out, too. Reluctantly, I followed.

Debbie, Anna Maria, Elizabeth, Amy, Laurie, and Trish gathered around us. Their voices sounded too loud now that we were
away from the Fall Fling. The night air chilled my skin.

"What now?" Anna Maria said. "Should we, like, just walk up
and ring the doorbell?"

"We could throw rocks at her window," Debbie said. She
mimed an overhand pitch. "Ker-rash!"

"She'd think it was a gunshot," Elizabeth said, snickering.

A thread of fear moved through my chest. I glanced up at the
house, which was completely dark, and I remembered what Mary
Bryan had told me.

Bitsy and Camilla were neighbors.

I turned to Mary Bryan. "Why are we here?"

She avoided my eyes. "Don't worry. Nothing's going to happen."

"They're talking about smashing her window," I said.

"Nobody's smashing anybody's window," Bitsy said. "We just
felt sorry for her, right, girls? All alone on the night of Fall Fling."
She draped her arm over my shoulders. "Heartbreaking, really.
She's in desperate need of human contact."

I shoved her off. "Her parents will call the police. The second
they see you, they'll call the police."

"Hmm," Bitsy said, tapping her lip. "No, don't think so, luv. Her
parents are out with my mum, trying to keep up the charade that
they're still dear friends, even without my father to round out the
foursome. So Camilla's on her own, poor dear."

Anna Maria burped. She'd gotten the flask out again, and

schnapps dribbled down her chin. "Little Debs, get a rock," she said.

"What are we, a band of marauders?" Bitsy asked. "I said no rocks."

"Then what?" Anna Maria demanded.

Bitsy smiled. She looked at all of us, her gaze lingering longest on me. "I know where they keep their spare key."

Anna Maria hooted. "Yeah, baby! Let's get us some ho-bag ass!"

"Aren't we . . . aren't we going to wait for Sukie and Pammy?" Laurie asked. She alone seemed the slightest bit reluctant.

"Sukie's not coming," Bitsy said. "Pammy had to take her home."

"Why?" Laurie said.

"Sukie wasn't having much fun, let's leave it at that. But she'll be right as rain before you know it. Won't she, Jane?"

I swallowed. "What are you going to do? To Camilla."

"Nothing," Mary Bryan insisted.

Keisha looked grim.

"Oh, I don't know," Bitsy said. "What do you think, Anna Maria? What was that you told me about those boys at football camp? Somewhere in Florida, I think. Got into the papers and everything."

"I didn't tell you. You told me," Anna Maria said. Her words came out messy. "But yeah, how they held down some freshman and stuck a stick up his ass."

"Sick bastards," Bitsy said.

"Said they did it to toughen him up. And you were like, 'Poor little tyke, bet he was scared out of his mind.'"

"So true. What did he do to deserve it?"

"But Camilla, on the other hand . . ." Anna Maria said.

"Skank," Debbie said.

"Whore," Elizabeth contributed.

"Tight ass," Amy tossed out.

"Sometimes a girl like that needs a prod on the bum, yeah?" Bitsy said.

"Bitsy, stop it," Mary Bryan said. "You're being gross."

Bitsy rolled her eyes. "Good god, Mary Bryan, you're as bad as Jane. You don't think we're *serious*, do you?"

She led her henchmen up the drive, leaving me, Keisha, Mary Bryan, and Laurie behind. Anna Maria took a detour into the manicured yard, where she broke off a thick stick from an azalea bush.

"Anna Maria!" Debbie cried, as in, *You bad thing!* Sniggering, they ran to catch up.

Bitsy turned around. "Laurie? Aren't you coming?"

Laurie glanced at Keisha, who frowned. But when Keisha headed toward the house, Laurie followed. Mary Bryan, too, until I grabbed her arm.

"No," I said. "This is crazy."

"She's just fooling around," Mary Bryan said. "You know how she is."

"Yeah. Exactly." My muscles were shaky, because I knew how

quickly things could change. "What happened to you, me, and Keisha being, like, a force for the good?"

"I didn't see you doing anything to stop her," she pointed out.

"Well, you sure didn't either!"

The others were halfway up the driveway. Anna Maria and Debbie were leading an inane chant of "Kill the skank. Kill the skank," which Elizabeth and Amy gleefully took up. Bitsy laughed, but didn't join in.

A knot in the center of me heated up. I felt sick and I felt scared, but I felt angry, too. I started for the house.

"Don't," Mary Bryan said. "You're going to mess everything up."

I shook her off.

"We have to stay together!" Mary Bryan said. "All four of us, we have to stay together or it won't work. Don't you get that?"

"What won't work?" I demanded. "This? Bitsy's little games of torture?"

"Don't be an idiot," she said. "*Us.* The fix. Everything." She stepped closer. "People won't like you anymore."

I looked at her, and I finally got it. Mary Bryan was just as scared as I was, only for different reasons. She thought I was going to opt out. She thought I was going to stand up to Bitsy as a parting shot, and then walk away from their bullshit, leaving them crippled without their magic fourth. I would have laughed if everything hadn't been so completely shitty.

"I think what you mean is that people won't like *you* anymore,"

I said. "And you know what, Mary Bryan? I don't fucking give a damn."

"You will," she said.

"Whatever," I said. "At least I never had sex on a picnic table." I left her staring after me as I sprinted up the drive.

A white Range Rover was parked inside one half of the two-car garage. Adjacent to the garage was a stone pathway that led to the back of the house, and around the bend I could hear Anna Maria and the others. They were no longer making any effort to be quiet.

I hurried to the back door. "Move," I said, elbowing Amy in the gut.

"Hey, watch it!" she cried. Then she saw it was me and giggled. "Oh, sorry. Make way for Jane! Clear a path!"

I broke through to see Bitsy gazing at a second-story window, where a light shone from behind the curtains.

"Come now, Camilla," Bitsy cajoled. "Don't play hard to get. We just want to spend some quality time with you. Right, girls?"

"The skank loves dick!" the girls caroled. "The stick is dick!"

The curtains moved. Camilla's pale face appeared, then disappeared.

"She's going to call the police," I said, willing my voice to be steady.

Bitsy turned. "Why, look. If it isn't little Jane."

"Or if she doesn't, I will."

"You would, wouldn't you?"

I blushed. Debbie and Anna Maria sniggered, and my hands balled into fists.

"Just leave her alone," I said. "Maybe she's not, like, Miss Congeniality, but she never did anything to you."

"*So* not the point," Bitsy said. She jerked her head at a small ceramic poodle to the right of the back door. "Laurie, get the key. It's under there."

"Laurie, don't," I said.

Laurie, who had taken one step toward the poodle, stopped in her tracks.

"*Laurie,*" Bitsy said.

"I'll do it," Anna Maria said. "Jesus." She strode across the entranceway and kicked over the poodle, which shattered when it hit the stones. Underneath lay the key. "Nice hiding spot," she said as she bent to retrieve it. She chortled, her stupid azalea stick still clutched in her other hand. "Real sneaky, ho-bag."

For a flashing moment I felt absolute panic, because god help me, I wanted to join in. *The skank loves dick, the stick is dick . . .*

But I fought against it, because I was not going to be that person. Yes, I was a Bitch. But I didn't have to *be* a bitch.

I pushed past Bitsy and Laurie and up to Camilla's door, where Anna Maria was inserting the key in the lock.

"Give it to me," I said, grasping her wrist.

Debbie edged closer, as did Trish and Amy.

"Jane," warned Mary Bryan, who'd joined the rest of the group.

I thought I caught movement at the second-story window. Why hadn't Camilla called the police? Or if she had, where were they?

"Give it to me or I'll scream. I mean it. I'll scream so loud the neighbors will come running."

"What neighbors?" Bitsy asked. "*I'm* her neighbor."

"You're not the only one," I said.

She strolled toward me, trying to feign indifference despite the tightness in her jaw. I could feel the force of her hate.

"Anna Maria, unlock the door," she ordered.

Anna Maria twisted the key.

I screamed.

🐈

As Bitsy's thugs scattered, as Mary Bryan hissed, "For shit's sake!" and pulled Bitsy out of the back-porch light, I felt something claw my arm. Camilla. She yanked me inside and slammed the door.

"What did you do that for?" she demanded.

I pulled free and pressed my face against a side window. Keisha waited for Mary Bryan and Bitsy by the garage. Then all three fled down the driveway, high heels clattering. Bitsy's laugh floated through the night air.

Camilla's phone rang, a sharp, staccato blare. Camilla crossed the room and picked up.

"Hello?" she said. "No, everything's fine. I'm really sorry. I—" Her lips thinned. "Yes, Mr. Cutter. I understand. Good-bye."

She hung up. The phone rang again.

"Hello?" she said. "I know. I did, too. But it was just a joke, Mrs. Robinson. It was someone from my school. Okay. Okay. Bye."

She faced me. "Mrs. Robinson's, like, eighty years old," she said. "You practically gave her a heart attack. And Mr. Cutter would have called the police if I hadn't stopped him. Is that what you wanted?"

I stared at her.

She strode through the house, and after a moment's hesitation, I followed. She crossed a spacious foyer, opened the front door, and stepped outside. On the other side of the street, a man stood with his hands on his hips at the top of his driveway.

"What's going on over there?" he barked.

"It's all right, Mr. Simmons," Camilla called. "Everything's all right. Sorry!"

She shut the door and leaned against it. She hid her face in her hands.

"I didn't . . ." I said. "I never . . ." I shook my head, unable to process her reaction. "I was *helping* you."

"Gee, thanks," she said.

I straightened my spine. "Look, I just risked everything for you. Why didn't you call the cops?"

"And tell them what, that some girls in prom dresses were standing outside my house?"

"No, and tell them . . . I don't know. Tell them that—"

"Anyway, Bitsy would have oozed her charm all over the officers, and by the end it would somehow be all my fault. As usual."

She swiped her hand under her eyes in a fast, angry gesture. "And Monday at school everyone would hate me even more than they already do."

"No, they wouldn't," I said. "Anyway, so what? You don't care what they think."

The look she gave me suggested otherwise.

"You don't care what *anyone* thinks," I insisted.

"Yeah," she deadpanned. "That's right. So you can leave now, because you've done your good deed. You can trot home knowing that you're morally superior to Bitsy McGovern, which, I'm sorry, isn't saying very much." She moved so that she was no longer blocking the door. "See ya."

This was so not what she was supposed to be saying. I didn't know what she *should* have been saying, but not this.

"Camilla—"

"Thanks. Really. Now, bye."

My body hardened with bottled-up frustration. Didn't she get how screwed she was? How, save for the grace of me, she was dog shit on the bottom of Bitsy's gleaming black boots?

I kept my mouth shut for maybe a second, and then I lifted my chin and told her *everything*. About the stealing, about Lurl— practically everything. Camilla tried to resist, indicating her disbelief with snorts of scorn, but I dug in.

"*That's* why you're so unpopular," I said. I'd followed her into the kitchen, where she'd gone in an attempt to escape me. "*That's* why everyone treats you like scum, because Bitsy steals your popularity from you every single week. Don't you even care?"

Camilla's breath came short. A hidden anguish vibrated in her voice as she said, "Are you taping this? Do you have a video camera tucked beneath your armpit?"

I spread my arms. "I'm not taping anything. Jesus."

"Let's see your purse. Come on, I know you have one."

She darted toward me, and my veins surged with adrenaline. I clamped my elbows to my sides and twisted away. Otherwise I would have hit her. I swear I would have.

"They had a *key*, Camilla," I said. "Bitsy had your spare key, all right? They were going to come in."

She looked at me. I looked at her. I wanted to mention the stick, but some things can't be expressed.

"Well?" I finally said. "Aren't you going to say anything?"

"It wouldn't have worked. We had the lock changed."

"You had the . . . what?"

"Some pervert's been e-mailing me sex messages. He even called and invited me to a Zamfir concert. Are you going to blame that on hocus-pocus, too?"

I felt a sliding down of hope. I didn't believe the truth at first. Why should she?

But then I saw in her eyes that she *did* believe—or wanted to, anyway. She wanted it to be true, because at least then there would be an explanation of why life sucked so bad.

"I'll prove it," I said. "You can drive us to Lurl's office in your dad's Range Rover, and I'll show you."

She moved restlessly. "Show me what, exactly? You said Lurl's office was empty every time you went in. Or are you changing your story to lure me out of the house?" She returned to the front door and peered through a rectangular window. "Are they still out there, waiting by their cars?"

"Their cars are gone," I said. "You can see for yourself."

"Uh-huh. And you want me to steal my dad's car and chauffeur you over to the school so we can break into a teacher's office."

"It wouldn't be stealing. It would be borrowing." I realized that maybe I wasn't the one to be clarifying these finer moral distinctions, but I pushed on. "And we wouldn't have to break into Lurl's office. I already told you, I have a key."

"*If* the school is even unlocked."

"It will be. Fall Fling, remember?"

Camilla still didn't trust me. But she didn't order me out, either.

"When would we do it?" she said. "Right now? This very second?"

She said it like a challenge, but I knew that if we waited until morning, it would never happen.

"Right now," I said. "This very second."

The Range Rover was an automatic, but still Camilla manhandled both the gas and the brake to the point that I had to wrap my arms around my stomach.

"It's not my fault," she said. She glanced at me defiantly, but her mouth was tight and pale. "I don't have driver's ed until next year."

I doubt it'll help, I wanted to say. But I didn't. I directed her to my house, where I snuck upstairs to get the key to Lurl's office and a few other last-minute items.

When I got back in the car, Camilla took one look at the object in my hand and said, "What's that for?"

"Don't worry about it," I said. I fingered the jade comb and thought about the me that used to be, before all this happened.

"And the . . ." She gestured at my quilted cotton vest, which I'd slipped on over my party clothes. Its sunshines danced ludicrously across my chest. "Why are you wearing that?"

I twisted my body and stared out the window, because if I couldn't explain it to myself, then how could I explain it to her? I wasn't sure why I'd put it on, just that it seemed like the right thing to do. I was glad that the J pendant and the teddy bear were out of sight in the backpack I'd grabbed from my desk.

"And *I'm* the school freak," Camilla said under her breath. "Yeah, makes a lot of sense."

"Just drive."

The school's parking lot was empty, save for a beat-up Pinto that I knew belonged to Angie Clark, president of the pep club. Down at the gym, Angie and a few of her buddies were probably taking down streamers and loading up trash bags. But Hamilton Hall was deserted.

"Are we going in or not?" Camilla said.

"Chill," I said. A breeze shook the leaves in the trees, making a dry rustling sound that made me think of bones. The building was right there, only yards away, but my legs stayed planted where they were. It was as if my body knew something that I didn't.

The wind rose, ruffling my hair, and I quick stepped forward to the basement door. I did a fancy move with the jade comb, and the door sprang open. Although it would have anyway, since the door wasn't bolted. My lock-picking was just for show.

"Well?" Camilla said.

I took off my heels—too loud—and shoved them into my backpack. Then I slipped barefoot into the unlit building. The yellow on my vest was dimly visible, and Camilla eyed it again and blew air out of her mouth.

"I can't believe you wore that to school," she said.

"What? I never wore this to school."

Camilla gazed at me. "We *are* at school."

I pressed my lips together.

"Third floor—that's where Lurl's office allegedly is, right?" she said. She marched down the hall. "We better get a move on."

Ceiling-level fire alarms shone faintly, casting an eerie red light over the rows of lockers. In the stairwells, moonlight streamed in from square windows. What looked normal by day was claustrophobic by night, full of hungry shadows stretching toward us as we padded toward Lurl's office. Or as I padded, rather. Camilla walked normally, spine erect and arms swinging. I admired her for it even as I resented it.

On the third floor, I banged my shin against what turned out to be a wire Animal Control cage. "Fuck," I said. Pain bloomed under my skin, and I paused to massage my muscle. Camilla stopped, too, turning around when she realized I was no longer with her, and in the sudden quiet I heard a scrabbly sound. Like claws tic-tacking across the floor.

Clamminess squeezed my insides. "Do you hear that?" I whispered.

"Hear what?" Camilla said in her normal voice.

"Shhh," I said. I strained my ears, but the noise was gone. We continued on. We reached the corridor that connected the north hall to the south hall, and looking at the heavy door, I was again hit with foreboding. I didn't want to go on.

Camilla exhaled impatiently.

I tugged it open, and we stepped into the dark passageway. This section had neither windows not fire alarms, so when the door thunked shut behind us, we were thrown into black. My body went rigid.

"Open it back," Camilla said beside me. Her voice slipped higher up the register. "I can't see a thing."

I scrambled for the handle. At first I couldn't find it, and my panic mounted. Then my fingers found purchase, and I pushed the door open to let in a sliver of gray.

"Use your shoe to prop it," Camilla said.

"Use *your* shoe," I said, still feeling freaked and hoping it didn't show. But my shoes, safe in my backpack, were delicate silver sling-backs. Hers were some weird kind of sneakers involving velour.

She made as if to return to the main hall. "Fine. Guess it's not that important to you after all."

"Wait," I said. I fumbled in my pack, pushing my shoes aside, and grasped the teddy bear. I jammed it between the door and the frame.

The corridor was still dark, but not *as* dark, and the quality of the light gave the night a kind of dreamlike unreality. I hesitated, then walked to Lurl's office. I really didn't want to do this, but I had the dreadful sense that it was the only way.

I drew the key from my pack. "Okay," I said. "Here goes."

"Here goes nothing," Camilla said.

I turned the key in the lock. I twisted the knob.

A yowl pierced the air, and a mass of fur and muscle drove into my chest. I yelped and tried to get it off me, but its claws dug into my quilted vest.

"Help!" I cried. I pried one paw free, only to have the cat latch back on and climb higher on my shoulder. "Camilla! *Do* something!"

The cat howled. I shoved. Digging my hands under its front legs, I flung it to the floor. It scrambled to its feet and trotted back over. It meowed and butted my leg. A rumbling purr started up in its chest.

"He likes you," Camilla said.

I breathed hard and examined my vest, now scratched and ripped. "This would have been my skin," I said. "I would have been, like, shredded."

Camilla strode into Lurl's office and flicked on the lights. One of the bulbs popped and went out, leaving us in half-lit dusk.

"So where's the great mystery?" she said, scanning the barren room. "You better not have dragged me here just for this."

I moved forward, but the cat twined between my legs and made me trip.

"Goddammit," I said.

The cat stretched on its hind feet and attempted to scale me. I winced as it pawed my bruised shin.

"Quit it. I mean it—quit it!"

"I don't see anything," Camilla said. She turned to leave.

"Will you just give me a minute?" I snapped. I shook the cat from my leg and tugged the J pendant out of my pack. I jerked the cord, and the J danced. The cat meowed and batted it with its paw.

"You want this?" I said. "Huh?" I dangled the pendant down low and dragged it across the floor. I slung it down the hall, and the cat skittered after it. I closed the door.

"Okay," I said. "All right."

"All right, what?" Camilla said.

I pointed to the office's rear door, the one that led to what I knew must be an empty storage room. Or who knows, maybe not so empty. "In there. It's got to be."

"*What's* got to be?" she said. But she crossed the room, and I followed. For a moment, she wavered. Then she opened the door.

"Holy shit," she said.

My blood reversed directions in my veins. Staring from the shadows were corpses, mute and still. Then my brain caught on, and I realized they weren't corpses—of course not corpses, why had I thought corpses?—but lifesize goddess figures. The room was packed with them. A rough stone goddess with arms out-spread stood by a marble goddess with a swollen belly. A black Aphrodite. A lifesize Kali, goddess of death and resurrection, with her ever-present string of skulls around her neck.

"What the hell . . . ?" I whispered. The light filtering in from Lurl's office wasn't much, but as my eyes began to adjust, I made out bits and bobs of brightness in the gloom. A butterfly barrette sparkled from an ivory snake goddess. A tiny mirror was tucked among the skulls on the figure of Kali. A heavy-breasted goddess held Alicia's lip balm in her upturned limestone palm.

"Do you believe me now?" I asked. "Can we get out of here?"

Camilla was pale.

"That's my headband," she said. She snatched a creamy suede headband from a statue sculpted to look like the Egyptian goddess Isis. "And that's my necklace! I looked everywhere for that neck-lace!" She ripped a chain off the tip of a crescent moon, which an alabaster goddess lifted to the heavens.

"Camilla," I said. "Come on, don't mess it up."

She stared at me incredulously. She strode across the room,

careless of the offerings she knocked out of place, and reclaimed a silver bracelet. From its links dangled a heart-shaped charm, etched with a B for ballet.

"Stop," I pleaded. "This isn't cool."

"Is there anything else?" she demanded.

I thought of the bobby pin. "No."

"Are you sure?"

"There's nothing else, I swear."

We heard a noise, and both of our heads swung toward the source. There. A stain in the darkness.

Camilla rejoined me in a series of jackrabbit steps. The Isis figure tottered as she passed, and a collection of bracelets clinked to the floor.

"What's over there?" she asked.

"I don't know," I said. "How should I know?"

Our voices were strained.

"Go look," she said.

"What? *You* go look."

We stared into the shadowy corner. A shape shifted almost imperceptibly. There was a muted thump.

My heart rose in my throat, and I whispered, "Where's the light? There's got to be a light for this room, too." I turned from the shape and found the switch. I flicked it, but nothing happened.

"It's a cradle," Camilla said.

I faced it again. Terror fluttered in my chest.

"Go look," she commanded. "Or I will."

Everything inside me grew dizzy, and I blamed her. Who was she to throw out a dare? Who was she to imply that she was the one in charge?

I forced my feet to move. The goddess figures seemed to watch me as I approached—it was like being in a room filled with menacing strangers—and the air grew unpleasantly warm. I smelled cat shit and old pee. I stepped closer, and the shape in the corner gained definition. Yes. A cradle, small and worn. A thump as its rockers met the floor.

I peered inside.

A litter of kittens nuzzled against their mother, kneading her torso, butting their heads on her abdomen, suckling her belly.

No.

Not suckling.

A kitten shifted its body, and I saw a flap of the mother's fur. Another kitten tugged at the flap, and it came off way too easily. Tiny teeth dug into the flesh below.

My eyes strayed higher, and I spotted the incision across the mother's neck. I must have cried out, because a snow white kitten lifted its head and looked at me. Its pupils were vertical slits. It returned to lapping the clotted blood, and a littermate nosed closer, eager for its share. The cradle rocked harder. A thump and a thump. And under the thumping, something else. A growl, low and menacing. It seemed to come from the walls.

I stumbled back the way I had come. "Let's go," I said. *"Now."*

I fled Lurl's temple and retreated through the outer office. I knew I should go back and put everything in order, but all I wanted was to be gone. Gone, gone, gone—and away from what I wished I'd never seen.

"Could you maybe speed it up just the tiniest bit?" I said. I jiggled from foot to foot. Camilla was too far behind me.

"Could you maybe relax?" she retorted. "This was your idea, in case you've forgotten."

She flipped off Lurl's light and followed me into the hall. She slammed the door behind us.

In the Range Rover, the reality of what I'd done sunk in.

"You can't tell anyone," I told Camilla.

She pressed down on the accelerator. "Who would I tell?"

"I'm serious. What you saw is, like, top secret. I will be in so much trouble if you blab."

She didn't respond. I hadn't articulated what I'd seen in the cradle, and I wasn't about to. But the rest—the goddess figures, the offerings, the low growl which Camilla must have heard—that knowledge alone was enough to make Camilla dangerous.

My fingers found the ripped part of my vest and closed around it. I tried to think without freaking out. I tried to think how to make this all be okay.

"And don't worry about . . . you know," I said. "Because I'm going to fix things. Fix them for you, I mean. I'll tell Bitsy that she can't steal from you anymore—but only if you promise not to mess things up."

She glanced at me skeptically.

"Plus, now you know to be on the lookout, so she wouldn't be able to steal from you even if she tried." I lifted my chin. "So you pretty much owe me."

She pulled up in front of my house. She gazed out the driver's side window.

"Why does she hate me so much?" she asked.

"What? She doesn't *hate* you. She just . . ." A prickle of heat spread on my neck. "She doesn't hate you."

"You don't have to lie. Anyway, I hate her, too, so we're even."

I fidgeted. They were hardly even.

"When you hate someone, you think about her all the time," Camilla said. She traced a faint white line of bird shit on the other side of the window pane. "You become obsessed."

Oh, just shut up, I thought. But what I said was, "Well. . . that's all over, because like I said, I'm going to make it stop. It's all going to stop."

She turned to face me.

"So do you promise you won't go tattling to the whole school?" I said. "Not that anyone would believe you."

An opaque look appeared in her eyes, then slid away. She released her breath in a slow letting go. "I won't go tattling."

I felt a tremendous gush of relief. Gratitude, even, despite the fact that she was the one who should feel grateful to me.

That night I dreamed of a mouthless kitten. As in, no mouth where the mouth should be. Just a knob of fur. I reached to pet it—poor little thing—and a mouth yawned into being with a terrific snap. It latched onto my hand with tiny sharp teeth, and I couldn't shake it off. Its body was warm and pulpy.

I awoke with a gasp and knew I had to go back. I didn't want to, more than anything I didn't want to, but I knew I had no choice. I had to return to Lurl's office and straighten everything up, and hopefully Lurl wouldn't notice that Camilla's things were missing, at least not right off the bat. Then I would leave, and it would all be behind me.

So after breakfast—during which Mom asked if I had a good time at the Fall Fling, and I answered, "Uh-huh"—I dumped out the contents of my backpack to find my key. But the key wasn't there. My pulse accelerated, and I riffled through the contents again. Kleenex, a smushed Mike and Ike box, a couple of tarnished pennies. But where else could it be? I'd unlocked the door, the tomcat had attacked, and—*shit.*

I must have left the key in Lurl's lock, where it would be sitting in what was now plain daylight. Yet another reason to get over there before anyone else came along.

I dragged my bike out of the garage and pumped hard all the

way to school. I used the basement door, same as before, and rushed up the stairs to the third floor. It was easier with the sun streaming through the windows. It was easier, in the light, to push aside thoughts of cats in the walls.

I opened the heavy door that led to the rarely used corridor, and by the baseboard I spotted my teddy bear. I scooped it up and scanned the floor for the J pendant, but the floor was bare. The cat must have run off with it.

I approached Lurl's office, and I felt a sudden hollow rush in my chest. *No,* I prayed. *Please, no.*

The door was locked. My key was gone.

My first thought was Bitsy. She'd one-upped me again, and now she was going to hold it over me to make me sweat. Or maybe it was Keisha? Maybe she'd sensed something was up and trailed me for the sake of damage control. Good ol' Keisha, always the worry-wart. And in this case it had paid off.

Or shit, maybe it was Lurl. Maybe she'd made a midnight jaunt to her shrine, maybe only minutes after Camilla and I left. I got the heebie-jeebies thinking about it. What if she'd lurched in on us? I couldn't imagine what she'd have done.

My bike jounced over a bump, and I tried to focus on the road. But my mind was too busy conjuring up possibilities. Lurl with the key. Mary Bryan with the key, which wouldn't be *so* bad. Everyone yelling at me. The kittens' frantic hunger.

Bottom line, I'd screwed up. *Bad Jane. Naughty, naughty girl.*

But whoever had my key would have to give it back, even if they punished me for it first in some stupid way. Because for the Bitches to exist, there had to be four.

ᴥ

"Keisha!" I called out when I saw her the next morning. I jogged to her locker. "Thank god. I ran into Mary Bryan on the front stairs, and she cruised by me without even saying 'hi.' I mean, obviously she must not have seen me, but it made me paranoid. But everything's good, right?"

Keisha's eyes flew to mine, then away. She focused on filling her backpack.

"I know I pissed her off," I said. "I maybe, you know, said some things I shouldn't have. But she's not *ignoring* me, is she?"

"Jane . . ." Keisha said.

My muscles tightened. Still, I pulled my mouth into a smile shape. "What? Are you pissed, too? I'm *sorry*, okay? Throw me in the chokey. Feed me to the dogs."

Keisha closed her locker. The look she gave me was sad, not angry, and she said, "I wouldn't have let anything happen, you know. At Camilla's."

"Oh, I know," I said. "I *totally* know. And I guess I was, like, overreacting or whatever. But that doesn't—"

Keisha walked away, leaving me talking to nobody.

ᴥ

After homeroom, I hunted down Mary Bryan. I felt bad about my picnic table comment, and I wanted to apologize. She would try to stay aloof, but she'd relent despite herself. And then she'd give me some answers.

I skipped English to talk to her, because I knew on Mondays she had first period free. I found her on the steps of Hamilton. She was wearing a pale blue sweater that matched her eyes.

"Are you mad at me?" I asked.

"Me?" she said. She kept her expression neutral. "Why would I be mad?"

Fine, I thought. *Let her get it out of her system*. "Because I just wanted to say I'm sorry," I said. "I didn't mean to hurt your feelings."

She gazed at me. Then, in a voice as bland as her expression, she said, "Okay, thanks." She returned to her algebra.

I didn't know quite what to do. Was that it? Was I forgiven? It didn't feel as if I was forgiven.

"It was just a really bad night," I said. "I was totally stressed out. Obviously. And then after you guys left, even *more* stuff happened"—I watched for her reaction—"and now it's like, *whoa*, my head is totally spinning, you know?"

Nothing. Not a flicker of an eyelid. But she had to know what I referring to, because somebody had my freaking key.

"Mary Bryan . . ."

She lifted her head. She smiled her nice-girl smile, the one she gave everyone. "I'm really kind of busy. I've got a math test, and I'm *so* unprepared." She wrinkled her nose, her cute little show of *we're all in this together*, and my chest constricted.

"Mary Bryan, come on," I said. I heard how my voice sounded, and my heart beat faster. I nudged her toe. "Mary Bryan!"

"Ex*cuse* me?" she said. Gone was the buddy act. She looked at me as if I were trash.

My face flamed. "I'm sorry. I'm *sorry*, okay? Why are you shutting me out?"

"I have a *math* test," she said. "I'm sorry if you're feeling fragile, and I'm sorry I can't rub your tummy and make everything all better. But I have to study."

I backed away.

Something was terribly, terribly wrong.

With Bitsy, my exchange was as stupid and pointless as I should have known it would be. Which I *did* know it would be, but which I convinced myself of otherwise, out of sheer desperation.

Me: Bitsy, hold up. We need to talk.

Bitsy: Why, Jane, aren't you adorable. Is that a new shirt you're wearing?

Me: What? I'm not . . . I just need you to . . . Just listen, okay?

Bitsy: Well, something's different, I just know it. Is it your hair?

Me: Drop the act, Bitsy. I know you're all mad or whatever, but I also know that you need me. So play your little game if that's what you need to do, but get real: You're nothing without me.

Bitsy, laughing: Oh, pet. I think you've got it backward.

Me: You have to have four. You have to.
Bitsy: How sweet of you to care. Ta, now!

As she made her parting remark, she actually patted me on the head. Then she breezed off in her flippy lime-green skirt, her doggy-ears bouncing with every step.

As for Camilla, the one time I saw her was before fourth period, as I was on my way to French. Camilla was on the quad talking to Sukie Karing, which struck me as odd until I remembered that Sukie, like Camilla, was one of *them* now, at least temporarily. One of the toads.

Still, I paused to stare. Camilla usually kept to herself, her spine ballerina stiff and her nose in a book. But today she had the look of someone wearing a fancy new outfit, both self-conscious and proud. A funny little smile played around her mouth, and real words went back and forth between her and Sukie. At one point Sukie even laughed—and not in a mean way.

Well, whoop-de-do for Camilla, I thought. I guess our midnight jaunt had upped her confidence after all.

I started across the quad, then stopped, a half-formed thought itching at the back of my brain. A thought I never would have had if not for my crappy day, what with the Bitches' weird behavior. And now Camilla, gesturing with pale hands as she wooed a willing Sukie.

This was not the normal Camilla. There was nothing normal here at all.

I flashed back to the hallway outside Lurl's office, when Camilla and I had made our hasty escape. *Camilla* had turned off Lurl's lights. *Camilla* had shut the office door.

Nausea slammed into me. It wasn't Lurl who had taken my key, and it wasn't any of the Bitches. And it wasn't the cat who had taken my pendant.

It was Camilla.

"Give it back," I said. I held out my open hand.

Camilla was still flying high from her success with Sukie, but she slid a mask over her satisfaction.

"No," she said.

I floundered for a few seconds, then narrowed my eyes. *"Yes,"* I said. "It's mine. My dad gave it to me. And you took it. That's stealing, you know."

"Oh, please," Camilla said. She headed toward Hamilton Hall.

"Hey. *Hey!* I'm talking to you!"

She didn't turn around.

I ran to catch up. "I stood up for you that night. They were going to . . . and I stopped them, I told them no, and . . ." I grabbed her arm. "I'm the only reason you know anything about this in the first place. I did it to *help* you!"

Camilla's smile returned. "Believe me, you did."

The next day, Miriam Fossey told me my neck was dirty. Elizabeth Greene sloshed her Diet Coke down the front of my shirt, and Pammy Varlotta, when I sidled up next to her by the vending machines, blushed and refused to meet my gaze.

"You don't understand," I told her. "I'm the same person I used to be, I swear. It's just that the Bitches, they have this secret power, see? Well, actually, it's Lurl the Pearl who has the power, but she can't do it without them, and—"

Pammy bolted. She grabbed her granola bar and ran, while the kids behind me watched and snickered.

"There's nothing wrong with me!" I cried.

"That's debatable, I must say," muttered Rutgers Steiner, shoving quarters into the soft-drink dispenser.

During PE I approached Debbie, since I knew how much she hated Camilla.

"And now I get it," I explained. "Because I see her for the traitor she really is. And that's good, right? You believe me, right?"

She slammed an oversized red rubber ball into my chest.

"Don't go bad-mouthing Camilla," she warned. She caught the ball on the rebound and bounced it off my head. "Whining loser!"

Coach Shaw blew her whistle. "You're out, Goodwin! Take the bench!"

During my free period, I marched up to Mary Bryan in the commons area. I stood in front of her, hands on my hips, until she looked up.

"This is ridiculous," I said. "This is absurd."

"This is life," she said. She went back to her fingernails, carefully applying lavender flower decals over a pearly pink base coat. When I kept standing there, she said, "Pardon me, but you're in my light."

When lunchtime rolled around, I retreated to the library. I needed to be away from everybody. I needed time to figure things out.

"Hello, Jane," Ms. Cratchett said, looking up from a stack of index cards.

"Hi, Ms. Cratchett," I said. Was it my imagination, or was even she regarding me a little frostily? I surprised myself by approaching her desk.

"So . . . are you still having problems with those cats?" I asked.

Her mouth creased in displeasure. "It's a travesty. Cat hair all over my keyboard, and this morning, excrement by my coffee pot. Excrement! It's getting so they think they own the place."

I nodded sympathetically, not knowing exactly where I was going but plunging forward nonetheless. "You should see Ms. Lear's class—they're seriously *everywhere*. Poor Ms. Lear, huh?"

"Lurlene?" Ms. Cratchett said. "Lurlene doesn't give a damn, pardon my French. I've told her, 'Come see the mess they made of my periodicals. Then try telling me they're your furry little beasties.'"

"She calls them her furry little beasties?"

Ms. Cratchett pursed her lips. She shuffled her index cards.

"Don't you have work to do? Don't you need to trot off to your hidey-hole and pretend to be busy?"

I blinked. Her frostiness was *not* in my imagination. Even so, I made myself push on.

"But about Ms. Lear . . ."

"Yes?"

I didn't actually know what I wanted to ask. *Is she a mad-woman? What does she do in that back room, in that eerie, ghoulish temple? Why does she smell like tuna?*

Finally, I said, "How long has she been here, anyway? At Crestview."

Ms. Cratchett cackled in an on-the-brink kind of way. It occurred to me that she should probably consider new employment. "Since the dawn of time—that's why she's got her claws in so deep. She was a student here herself, you know."

My stomach dipped. "Ms. Lear went to school here? As a student?"

"Not too bright, are you?" Ms. Cratchett said. "I suggest you try studying sometime instead of reading your dog-eared baby books. Now, shoo!" She flapped her hand at me. "Go on!"

I backed away from her desk, then made a beeline for the far bookshelves, over in the "Alma Mater Pride" section. There were old yearbooks there. Rows and rows of them.

How old *was* Lurl, anyway? It was impossible to tell. I flipped through 1979, then tried 1973, then 1972. Bingo. "Lurlene Lear," it said in the index. And then a listing of the pages she appeared on.

Dread made my limbs feel heavy. Did I really want to look? Then again, what choice did I have?

I sat on the floor and turned to page forty-eight, where I found Lurl's class picture in the senior section. If she wasn't labeled by name, I wouldn't have recognized her. She was beautiful, with glossy brown hair and glowing skin. She wasn't wearing glasses, and her eyes were luminous. A strand of creamy pearls circled her neck.

I flipped to another page. "Big Kid!" read the caption, and the picture showed Lurl reclining on one of the benches outside Hamilton Hall. She wore a baseball cap pulled low, and she was grinning at the camera. The print beneath the picture said, "Senior Lurlene Lear relaxes between classes. She'll always be a kid at heart!"

I looked at one more. This one was a full-page spread of a beaming Lurl wearing a tiara and clutching a bouquet of white roses. She was in Crestview's gym, I could tell, although it had been transformed by silver icicles and sparkling silver trees. A banner draped behind her said ENCHANTMENT IN THE SNOW.

I read the paragraph beneath the picture. "Lurlene Lear shines as Ice Maiden of the Winter Carnival. 'I am so blessed!' gushed Lurlene as she accepted her crown. 'I will never be happier in my whole entire life!'"

I closed the yearbook. I felt ill. How could Lurl have been . . . ? And how could she now be . . . ? What had *happened* to her? What had she turned into? And what the fuck was the deal with the cats?

I exchanged the '72 yearbook for the '71 one and checked out Lurl as a junior. Younger, and with shorter hair, but just as pretty and just as busy. One picture showed her on a hayride. "Yehaw!" read the caption.

In the '70 yearbook, Lurl as a sophomore cuddled a fluffy white cat, their cheeks pressed together. The cat looked vaguely panicked in that way animals do when they're held too tight. "Awww, how sweet!" were the words underneath, and then a bit about Lurl's volunteer work for the Humane Society. I didn't like looking at that one, and I shut the yearbook right away.

I pulled down the yearbook from 1969. In this one Lurl would be a freshman, just like me. Only when I checked the index, there was no "Lurlene Lear." There was a "Sandra L. Lear" listed, but no "Lurlene."

Something stilled within me, and the page numbers went out of focus. Sandra L. Lear. Sandy. The girl who had died?

My stomach turned upside down. I blinked to get my eyes working again and flipped to page twenty-three, the sole listing for Sandra L. Lear. And there she was, in the small rectangular box that framed her class photo. She stared out blankly, with no expression giving life to her features. Her eyes were dark empty holes.

Sand in the oyster—the thought came unbidden. And what had Lurl said? "Because I'm such a gem."

The stillness inside me broke into a million pieces, because Sandy hadn't died after all. She had just . . . changed. And come back as Lurl.

I stood up, letting the yearbook spill to the floor. I walked quickly out of the library and headed for the cafeteria. I broke into a run. I had the sense that someone was following me, and my nerve endings jangled with adrenaline. I had to tell people about this. I had to let them know.

But when I got to the lunchroom, I stopped at the door and stood there, panting. Because there was Camilla, sitting with the Bitches at the soccer jocks' table. Her face was glowing. Her eyes were luminous. She said something that I couldn't hear, and Anna Maria punched her on the shoulder. Debbie gave her an affectionate noogie, and everyone laughed.

Okay, I thought that afternoon. *Fine.* There was a whole lot of wrongness going on, things that were sick and creepy and unnatural, but the past was the past and the future was now. And I wasn't about to roll over and play dead just because the Bitches wanted me to—no way. They didn't get to decide who I was. Only I got to decide that. And I was not going to be a freaking toad.

I went to the mall and bought a pair of shit-kicking black boots. They cost a fortune, and they were even cooler than Bitsy's. I wore them the next morning along with the denim mini-skirt from my coming-out party and a fuzzy white V-necked sweater. I looked hotter than hot.

I waited for Nate at his locker, because what had Mary Bryan said? *He's yours if you want him. He wants to be your prince.*

Well, today was Nate's lucky day. I was finally going to make it easy on the poor guy.

I leaned sideways against the locker, my hip cocked and one arm up so that my sweater stretched over my chest. Then I decided that was a little too come-hither, so I switched positions and propped my back against the locker's metal grates, my arms folded over my ribs. I saw Nate come in through the front entrance, and a sick, zingy feeling started up inside me.

Relax, I coached myself. *Feel the power.*

"Hi," I said as he approached. "What's up?"

He seemed surprised to see me, but he didn't shut me out.

"Not much," he said. "You?"

"Oh, you know, just life as normal."

His eyes darted down the hall, which could have been wariness or could just have been nerves. I tried to remember to breathe.

"So anyway," I said, "I was just wondering . . . I mean, if you aren't busy or anything . . ."

He stepped nearer, his body *this* close.

"Hey," he said. He leaned in.

My pulse accelerated. I'd never been a fan of public displays of affection, but maybe that was because they'd never been directed at me. I wet my lips and tilted my head. "Yeah?"

"You're blocking my locker. Can you move?"

"Oh! Right. Sure." Heat spread through my body as I scooted out of the way. "So do you want to do something sometime?"

He shook his head. "Nah."

"But . . . I thought you liked me."

He shoved his books into his backpack and turned to leave.

No. This was not the way it was supposed to happen. I grabbed his shoulders and aimed for his lips.

"Sick!" he yelped, pushing me off.

I sprawled to the floor, and my mini-skirt slid high on my thighs. Some sophomore almost wet himself in delight.

"Nice crotch shot," he crowed. *"Not!"*

My humiliation that day included, but was not limited to, the following:

- my chair was pulled out from under me not once, not twice, but on three separate occasions;
- Miriam Fossey upended my backpack and kicked the contents across the floor;
- Ryan Overturf announced to the whole cafeteria that I'd be giving free blow jobs in front of Nate's locker, after which Nate shoved his shoulder and said, "Shut up, man. Don't give her any ideas.";
- and a cat pissed on my locker.

Oh, and in my early religions class, Lurl couldn't stop giggling. She'd teach a little, look at me, and let out her low, throaty man giggle. And I wasn't the only one freaked out by it. Everybody was.

"God dang," Bob Foskin stage whispered from the front row. "Stop setting her off, girl. Are you in heat or something?"

I sank lower in my seat. My foot hit something soft, and I jerked it back. A white cat hissed and swiped at my ankle, and my heart knocked against my ribs.

I drew my legs all the way up in my chair. I tried very hard not to think about kittens. But Lurl was right there, not ten feet away, and I searched her face for any clue about how she got to be who she was today. From the hollow-eyed freshman to the radiant Ice Maiden to . . . this. What unseen power had transformed her so completely?

She caught me looking, and she broke off her explanation of fertility and the blood of life.

"The devil's in the details, dearie," she said, pitching her words at me. She covered her mouth and dissolved into giggles.

As I was walking home from school, Alicia's sister Rae pulled up beside me in her Plymouth Cougar. She rolled down her window and called, "Hey. Jane."

I looked at her warily, and she threw a brush at me. A pink plastic Goody. She sped away, her horn blaring "Dixie."

On Thursday, I told Mom I was sick. I also told her that I needed to switch schools, because I didn't fit in at Crestview and I never would. I didn't mention the fact that my humanities teacher had sold her soul to the devil.

"Oh, honey," Mom said. She sat down beside me. "What's going on?"

"Nobody likes me. Everybody hates me."

"Guess you'll go eat worms?" she said, quoting a song she used to sing when I was little. She saw my death look. "Sorry. But, Jane, you've got tons of friends."

I pushed my Cheerios with my spoon.

"Don't you?" Mom asked. I snuck a look at her face and saw that she had grown uncertain. She started to rub my neck, then drew back her hand. "Surely things aren't as bad as you think."

"Yes, they are."

"Sweetie . . ."

I released my spoon handle. I watched it slide sideways under the milk.

Mom frowned. She glanced at her watch, then stood up. "Well, if you're really sick, you can stay home. But why don't you think about calling Alicia? Or Phil. Maybe they could cheer you up."

"Sure," I said. "That's a great idea."

Last week, Mom would have held my face in her hands and told me how much she loved me. Today, even she couldn't bear to touch me. I dumped my cereal into the sink and went back to bed.

I didn't go to school on Friday, either. What was the point?

No one called to check on me. No one brought me chicken soup.

In a fit of furious self pity, I threw away the teddy bear, the jade hair comb, and the Polynesian vest, as well as every other Dad-related knickknack I could find. I purged myself of everything

Dad, because what good had he done for me? He'd left on a three-year trek to find himself, and now, because of him, I was as lost as he was.

But I went back once my blood had cooled and dug out the teddy bear. I touched his stupid shirt, the one that said, "I Love Cairo." I hugged him tight, closing my eyes and resting my chin on his head.

That night, Mom went out with her friend Kitty. They were going to a ribbon-cutting ceremony at a boutique called "Essentials." There were going to be fabulous giveaways.

"Are you sure you don't mind?" Mom asked. "I'd be happy to stay home. We could order a pizza."

She would have, if I let her. I saw that now. But I said, "Go, I'll be fine. Really."

I watched Mom climb onto the back of Kitty's motorcycle, and I felt as if I were looking at her from a far back place inside of me. As if there were a gap between me and the rest of the world. Everything looked so fragile.

Kitty's voice rang out, and Mom laughed. She tightened the strap on her helmet.

Who are those people? I asked myself. *Who am I?*

Kitty's Harley purred to life, and I stood there until I could no longer see the taillights. I went back inside and picked up the phone.

First, I called Alicia. I was worried that Rae might answer, but she didn't.

"This is me," I said to the machine. "Jane. I need to talk to you, okay? Call me."

Next I called Camilla, but when Camilla's mom answered, she said Camilla was out for the evening.

"Oh," I said. "Uh . . . where?"

"A party," said Camilla's mom. I could hear the pride in her voice, the still surprise of it. "She dressed up as Dorothy from that movie with the munchkins. One of her new friends came by and helped her get ready."

"Right," I said, as if I'd simply forgotten. "Thanks so much."

On a hunch, I looked up Kyle Kelley's number and punched it in. I switched the phone to my other ear, wiped my palm on my jeans, and switched back. My pulse thrummed in my temples.

"Hello, gorgeous," Kyle said in a sultry tone. I heard voices and laughter in the background.

"Uh, hi," I said. Did he have caller ID? Did he know it was me? Just in case, I said, "This is Jane. What's up?"

"Who?" he said. The party noises were really loud.

"Jane," I said again.

"I'm sorry, do I know you?" he asked. There was a splintering crash, and he said, "For God's sake, Stuart, you're the tin man, not the terminator. Will someone please give this man some lubrication?" He came back to me full strength. "Who's this again?"

"It's Jane Goodwin. And I—"

"Nevermind sweets. This really isn't the best time. Bye now!"

The line went dead. I hit the off button and threw the phone onto the couch. It bounced off a cushion and landed on the floor, where it trilled its shrill ring.

I lunged for it. "Hello? Kyle?"

"No, it's Alicia," Alicia said. "Kyle who? Kyle Kelley?"

"Alicia, *hi*," I said. My chest opened with a rush of relief. "I'm so glad you called. It's been the most crappy week, I'm so not kidding."

"Uh-huh," she said. "What happened?"

"Well, your sister threw a hairbrush at me, for one. Can you believe it?"

Alicia didn't answer.

I quickly switched gears. "But the real thing is that they ditched me. The Bitches." I decided to lay it out for her, the whole of my shame, to make up for what I'd put her through. "They, like, totally dropped me, just like that, and now Camilla Jones is their new darling. Because she stole from *me*, can you believe it? So now she's a Bitch instead of me."

"Ha," Alicia said. "That's hysterical."

I laughed uncertainly. "Well, I wouldn't say hysterical, but—"

"And now you've gone from the top of the heap to the bottom. Lower than me, even, is that right?"

"What? You were never at the bottom of the heap. I mean, I'm sorry if you felt that way, but—"

"And where were you when I was so miserable? Were you there, holding my hand like a good friend should? No."

"I know," I said. "I'm sorry. I'm really, really sorry."

Alicia snorted. "That's for sure."

I wrapped my fingers tighter around the phone.

"Anyway, Tommy Arnez doesn't hate me anymore," she said. "We worked things out, just in case you were curious. He's picking me up in twenty minutes to go to a movie."

"Alicia, that's terrific," I said. I even meant it, figuring that the more she had on her side, the more likely she was to forgive me.

"Yeah. So I've got to go get ready."

"Oh," I said. "Right. Sure." I paused. "So . . . are we friends again? Not that we ever *weren't*, but you know what I mean."

For a few seconds, she didn't respond. Then she said, "Are you begging?"

"Am I . . . ? Alicia."

"*Are* you?"

"Do you seriously want me to?"

"Yes, actually. Very much."

I groaned. "Fine. I'm begging."

"Good," she said. "Now you know how it feels. And no, I'm not your friend, because even over the phone you make me want to vomit. I hope you rot in hell."

She hung up on me, making it twice in one night.

There was no point to living. There really wasn't. I spent all weekend attempting to convince myself I was better off without the Bitches, blah, blah, blah, and finally on Sunday morning I grabbed a jacket and headed for the park, just to escape my own stupid thoughts. The air was crisp, I could hear kids playing from a block away, and still my brain went around and around, obsessing over every last aspect of my downfall and trying to come up with reasons it was all for the best.

Such as:

I would no longer have to siphon off another girl's popularity to add to my own. No more stealing. And no more creepy Lurl and her cats.

I'd no longer have to watch Bitsy (or her thugs) bully Camilla, although any sympathy I'd had for Camilla was gone with the wind. Anyway, Bitsy would no doubt pick someone else to bully—probably me. And lucky Camilla would get to join in the fun.

As long as I was physically away from Mary Bryan and Keisha, I could tell myself—and even believe—that I wouldn't miss their two-facedness, their bright outer shells hiding the brokeness inside. But I knew, I *knew*, that as soon as I was around them, I'd fall back under their spell. Because that was how it worked. You got near them, and it was like being stroked. All you wanted was to please them, and have them like you, and it was like an ache, that's how bad you wanted it.

Tomorrow I should pin a card to my T-shirt, something only I could see. And it would say DON'T LIKE THE BITCHES! DON'T SMILE AND GIGGLE AND WAG YOUR TAIL! THEY ARE EVIL!

I'd have to steel myself against them. That's what Camilla must have done. All that time I thought she was immune, but she wasn't, because nobody was. She was just strong, that's all. And yet like an idiot I tried to rescue her, safe in her house with the changed lock that even Bitsy couldn't have opened.

Circle Camilla, cross out Jane.

I got to the park and claimed the one empty swing. A little girl with a ponytail swung beside me, or tried to. She knew how to pump, but she didn't know when. Her legs went out when they should have gone in, in when they should have gone out.

I gave her a sad little smile. She glowered.

"Jane!" someone called.

My head jerked up, and I searched past the swing set. "Phil?"

He held up a box of Krispy Kremes, the bottom splotched with grease. My heart raced. I didn't know if I was happy to see him or scared.

"What are you doing here?" I asked.

"I brought doughnuts," he said.

"So I see." I hopped off the swing, jittery with nerves.

He sat down under a tree and opened the box. "Still hot. Want one?"

I hesitated, then walked over and sat down. I lifted a doughnut from the box and took a bite. Sweetness melted through me.

"Your mom didn't know where you were," Phil said. "I figured here was as likely as anywhere."

I took another bite of doughnut. It amazed me that life could be so crappy, and yet a Krispy Kreme could taste so good. There was a very good chance I might cry.

Phil brushed a fleck of glaze from my lip. "You doing okay?"

His kindness undid me. My eyes welled with tears.

"Jane?" he said.

"Shut up. You hate me."

"No, I don't."

"Well, you should."

"Well, I don't."

I swiped the back of my hand under my eyes and sniffled. I choked down the now-gummy doughnut.

"How's Oz?" I asked.

"She's fine," he said. "How's Nate?"

I blushed. Did he know about the locker incident? How could he not? Instead of answering, I said, "So are you two a couple now?"

He looked at me in a way that made me feel ashamed. "She's not you, if that's what you're asking."

I dropped my eyes. I didn't know *what* I was asking, just that I needed someone not to find me abominable.

"I'm not a Bitch anymore," I confessed.

"You never were."

"You know what I mean. And now, instead of a Bitch, I'm a"— I took a shuddery breath—"a toad. I'm a toad, aren't I? You can admit it. It's not like I don't already know."

A snot bubble ballooned out of my nose. I sniffed it back in, and the utter patheticness of it made me sob out a laugh.

"Here, use this," Phil said, offering me a doughnut.

I looked at him. "To wipe my nose with?"

He shrugged.

I laughed again, this time more real. He leaned over—quick, as if otherwise he might chicken out—and kissed my cheek.

"There," he said. "I turned you back into a princess."

"Oh, you did, did you?"

"Janie."

"Phil."

He pulled me toward him, and I let him. I rested my head on his skinny chest. School tomorrow would be hell—as would the next day and the next day and the next. But he smelled like Krispy Kremes and Mennen Speed Stick, and leaning against him, I didn't feel so alone.

about the author

Lauren Myracle holds an MFA in Writing for Children and Young Adults from Vermont College. She lives in Colorado with her husband and three children.

Asked why she wrote *Rhymes with Witches*, Lauren said, "There's a book I love called *Flowers for Algernon*, by Daniel Keyes. (If you haven't read it, you should. It's great.) It's about a man named Charlie Gordon who has an operation that raises his IQ from 68 to 185, and at first Charlie's happy with the change. And then, well, he isn't. Because there's a price to pay for turning into someone new. There always is. Anyway, reading *Flowers for Algernon* made me wonder, what if there was a way to manipulate not intelligence but popularity? What if I was offered the chance to be popular beyond my wildest dreams—would I go for it? Would you? And if so . . . at what cost?"

This book was designed by Jay Colvin and art directed by Becky Terhune. It is set in Rotis Semi Sans, a typeface created by the German graphic designer Otl Aicher. Aicher is best known for the pictograms he designed for the 1972 Olympic Games in Munich. The display type is ITC Edwardian Script, designed by Ed Benguiat. Benguiat designed the typeface to mimic the effect of calligraphy written with a steel-point pen, which produces thick and thin strokes.

Enjoy this peek at Lauren Myracle's sequel
to her *New York Times* best-seller *ttyl* (talk to you later)

t t f n

(ta-ta for now)

---

ttfn

Saturday, November 20, 4:45 PM E.S.T.

SnowAngel:	hey there, zoe-cakes. r we studs or what? 😊
zoegirl:	ya-hootie!
SnowAngel:	i have a total adrenaline buzz going, even tho i am completely and thoroughly exhausted. my muscles r gonna be crazy sore tomorrow.
zoegirl:	i hear u. can u imagine how in shape we'd be if we did that every day?
SnowAngel:	we could call it the winsome-threesome workout-of-the-century. we could make an exercise video and rake in oodles of cash.

Send   Cancel

zoegirl:	even my toenails r tired
SnowAngel:	*flops onto pretend bed and groans*
SnowAngel:	i told chrissy what we did, and she was like, "u ran up the escalator at peachtree center? that super duper long one?"
zoegirl:	the critical point is that we ran up the *down* escalator. u did explain that to her, didn't u?
zoegirl:	that's gotta be the longest escalator in the world. seriously, it's as long as a football field.
SnowAngel:	i nearly lost it when maddie stopped for a breather and the escalator took her down, down, down. she was all, "noooo! i'm losing ground!"
zoegirl:	hee hee
SnowAngel:	but in the end we conquered it, cuz we can conquer ANYTHING, baby.
SnowAngel:	it's like my new favorite song, "run" by snow patrol. have i told u how much i love that song?
SnowAngel:	it goes, "light up, light up, as if u have a choice," and it's all about not giving in to the harshness of life even when everything's going against u.
zoegirl:	"as if u have a choice"? sounds sarcastic.
SnowAngel:	no, no, no, it's not. have u heard it?
zoegirl:	uh . . . no. is this another of those indie bands u discovered on your OC cd?
SnowAngel:	i discovered this one on my own, thank u very much. *pokes out tongue * the song is all melancholy and wistful, but at the same time beautiful and inspiring, and the lead singer's NOT being sarcastic. he's saying, "yeah, the world is hard, and maybe we don't have

Send   Cancel

	control, but we should ACT like we do. we should light up inside ourselves and shine."
SnowAngel:	i thoroughly agree, that's all.
SnowAngel:	and forgive me for sapping out, but the REASON i shine is cuz of u and mads. ☺☺☺
zoegirl:	awwwww
SnowAngel:	it's true. true blue, me and u, and don't forget to add maddie 2.
SnowAngel:	do u like my rhyme?
zoegirl:	very impressive
SnowAngel:	wait, there's more! er, let's c . . . since 7th grade they did not part, they stayed connected in their hearts. zoe's the good girl, maddie's wild, and sweet darling angela is meek and mild.
zoegirl:	meek? hahahahaha! mild? hahahahaha!
SnowAngel:	fine, miss brainiac. U find something to rhyme with wild.
zoegirl:	"and sweet goofy angela tends to act like a child"?
SnowAngel:	hey now!
zoegirl:	just teasing. u know i love u.
zoegirl:	i've just got kid-type ppl on my brain, cuz guess what? i got the job at Kidding Around!
SnowAngel:	wh-hoo! *happy dance, happy dance*
zoegirl:	there was a message waiting for me when i got home. i'm psyched.
SnowAngel:	ah, to be wiping noses and chasing toddlers. when do u start?
zoegirl:	um, don't freak, ok?
SnowAngel:	why would i freak? ur not gonna say something to

	make me freak, r u?
SnowAngel:	wait a minute. don't u DARE tell me u have to start tonite.
zoegirl:	the thing is . . . i do.
SnowAngel:	zoe! noooo!
zoegirl:	saturday nite's their busiest nite. the director wants me to come in for training.
SnowAngel:	but we were gonna watch "A Cinderella Story"! we were gonna freeze-frame the part where Hilary Duff goes into the locker room and has a fight with Chad Michael Murray!
zoegirl:	i know, and i will miss chad very much and pray that he understands. but we can have our "cinderella story" extravaganza tomorrow. that'll be even better, cuz that way maddie can actually join us.
SnowAngel:	the point being that she has plans tonite 2? yeah, rub it in. u've got ur job and maddie has her cousin's wedding and i have a big old pile of poop. thanks a lot.
zoegirl:	angela, u r such a drama queen.
SnowAngel:	☹
zoegirl:	ur not really mad, r u?
SnowAngel:	of course i'm mad! *flames shoot from ears *
SnowAngel:	only not really, cuz this way i can watch "extreme makeover: home edition" and no one will be here to make fun of me. and i will cry and it will be very emotional, and if u would just TRY the show then u would c what i mean.
zoegirl:	umm . . . no
zoegirl:	but u know what's weird? and i mean this in the nicest

Send   Cancel

	way ever. last year u would have been totally upset if i'd changed our plans at the last minute. i mean, truly upset, with all kinds of wounded hurt feelings. but this year, ur so much more chill. why is that, do u think?
SnowAngel:	cuz i'm a junior, that's why. *struts around in funky junior-ness* cuz i can drive, even tho i don't have a car. cuz i choose to light up, light up, even tho i will be all alone on a saturday nite, and even tho there is seriously something up with my parents, not that they'll admit it.
zoegirl:	there's something up with your parents? explain.
SnowAngel:	it's just this feeling i've been getting.
zoegirl:	like what? and for how long?
SnowAngel:	i dunno, maybe a week?
zoegirl:	a week?! why r u just now telling me???
SnowAngel:	it's like they're hiding something. i can't explain it better than that. i keep thinking that maybe i'm making it up, but then i think that i'm not.
zoegirl:	hmm, interesting
zoegirl:	maybe it's a *good* think they're hiding—like, that they're taking u to hawaii.
SnowAngel:	i dunno, that somehow doesn't seem very likely.
SnowAngel:	but, whatever. i'm not gonna worry about it, cuz i'm the new and improved Chill Angela. u think they would name a Barbie after me?
zoegirl:	definitely. and for the accessory, she could have a tiny iPod so she could listen to that "light up" song.
SnowAngel:	no, her accessory would be a tiny picture of u, me, and mads, cuz that's why i'm chill for real. cuz no matter

	what, i've got u guys giving me my me-ness. ☺
zoegirl:	maddie and i don't give u ur you-ness. u give urself ur you-ness.
SnowAngel:	"you-ness." now there's a word for u.
SnowAngel:	my granddad's name was eunice, btw
zoegirl:	grandDAD? u mean ur grandmom.
SnowAngel:	nope, my granddad. only he spelled it "unus."
zoegirl:	ugh. what were his parents trying to do to him?
SnowAngel:	his full name was unus faye. he went by U.F.
zoegirl:	i am so sorry to hear that.
SnowAngel:	yep
zoegirl:	well, on that note, gtg. wish me luck on my first day, which is really my first nite!
SnowAngel:	good luck on ur first day which is really ur first nite!
SnowAngel:	ta ta for now!

Send   Cancel

Saturday, November 20, 5:16 PM E.S.T.

SnowAngel:	hey, maderoo. getting all dolled up for ur cousin's wedding?
mad maddie:	**fyi, the dolling is done. fyi, i look fabu.**
mad maddie:	**the pops, however, has hit a new low.**
SnowAngel:	ooo, do tell
mad maddie:	**ahem. he bought this self-hair-cutter thing, right? cuz he's such a cheapskate that he didn't wanna fork over 10 bucks at lloyd's barbershop. and of course he decides that today, the day of donovan's wedding, is the perfect day for a trim. so i get home to find dad in the bathroom, hair-cutter aloft, and as i walk to my room, i hear the buzzing begin. bzzzzzzzzzzzzzz.**
SnowAngel:	what'd he do, give himself a mohawk?
mad maddie:	**if only. so then the buzzing stops, and he goes, "oops." "what happened?" i yell. and he says, "i put on the wrong attachment. guess my hair will be a little shorter than usual, huh?"**
SnowAngel:	uh oh
mad maddie:	**and then for some reason he starts asking if i have a safety pin or a needle or anything pokey. i think he was taking the whole thing apart. but no, i did not have anything pokey, so after a while he puts it back together and the buzzing starts again. and then it shuts off. and he starts LAFFING.**
SnowAngel:	oh, crap. what happened?
mad maddie:	**my idiot father forgot to put ANY attachment back on, which meant that when he started up again, he took off**

	an entire strip of hair down to his scalp. as in, bald. and then once he'd done that, he figured there was nothing to do but complete the scalping.
mad maddie:	**my father is a cue ball, angela.**
SnowAngel:	oh no!
SnowAngel:	that cracks me up that he would laff, tho. that's so ur dad.
mad maddie:	**he was all, "what? it's just hair." the moms is massively annoyed.**
SnowAngel:	if my dad went bald on the day of a wedding, my mom would jump out a window. or push HIM out a window.
mad maddie:	**ah, well. we'll go to the reception and drink away our troubles, cuz that's what my family does. should be a good time.**
SnowAngel:	that blows my mind that u can drink right there with them.
mad maddie:	**it's cuz we're irish. it's the law.**
SnowAngel:	my parents would be like, "u r underage. go sit at the kiddie table." but yours r like, "here, have another beer!"
mad maddie:	**well, they won't be the ones actually giving me beers. they'll leave that to my crazy aunts and uncles. and it won't be beer, it'll be champagne.**
SnowAngel:	la di da
mad maddie:	**and before long uncle duncan will be ranting about the iraqis and aunt teresa will be doing the line dance she learned in 8th grade to michael jackson's "beat it."**
mad maddie:	**i'm telling u, donovan's fiancee has noooooo idea what she's in for.**

SnowAngel:	sounds fun, tho
mad maddie:	**it definitely won't be boring**
SnowAngel:	do u wish—even just a little—that u and ian were still going out, so he could go with u?
mad maddie:	**not at all. ian is a fleck and i am a plane, high in the sky. that's how over him i am.**
SnowAngel:	swear?
mad maddie:	**ok, maybe not a plane. maybe just a . . . telephone pole.**
SnowAngel:	meaning what?
mad maddie:	**meaning that maybe i do miss him, but what's the point? if ian had wanted to come to donovan's wedding with me, then he shouldn't have broken up with me.**
SnowAngel:	he didn't break up with u. u broke up with him.
mad maddie:	**but only cuz i knew that he was going to. he called me a ball and chain, if u don't recall.**
SnowAngel:	WHAT?!!
SnowAngel:	he did NOT call u a ball and chain. he made that ONE comment about wanting to hang out with his friends more, and u did your porcupine thing where u bristle up over nothing.
mad maddie:	**there was more to it than that 1 comment. it was obvious i was cramping his style.**
SnowAngel:	omg. only u would interpret it like that.
SnowAngel:	it's ok to have feelings, u know. it's even ok to miss ian.
mad maddie:	**thanx for that, Dr. Phil.**
SnowAngel:	he adored u, mads. he would take u back in a heartbeat.
mad maddie:	**yeah, well, that boat's already sailed.**
mad maddie:	**that's nice of u to say, tho. u r so good to me.**

SnowAngel:	yup, cuz i luv ya
SnowAngel:	anyway, who knows? maybe tonite u'll meet someone new. maybe u'll meet your future husband!
mad maddie:	**or maybe NOT. i'm not looking for a husband, angela— sheesh!**
SnowAngel:	u never know . . .
SnowAngel:	so zoe got that job at Kidding Around, did u hear?
mad maddie:	**that's such a dorky name, Kidding Around. it's like, "hiya, buddy, watcha up to?" "not much—just kidding around." with everyone slugging each other on the shoulder.**
SnowAngel:	cuz it's a childcare place, for when parents don't have a babysitter or whatever. KIDDING around. get it?
mad maddie:	**der, angela. not getting it was never the problem.**
mad maddie:	**yikes, time to motor. old baldie's calling my name.**
SnowAngel:	have fun at the wedding! tell donovan congrats for me! OH, and u and zoe r both coming over tomorrow, ok? we're having Sunday Afternoon Movie Madness.
mad maddie:	**that sounds awesome—only not "A Cinderella Story." i am not watching u freeze-frame the locker room shot for the umpteenth billion time.**
SnowAngel:	we will take a vote
mad maddie:	**fine, we'll take a vote**
SnowAngel:	and my vote counts double since it's my house. ☺ buh-bye!

Send   Cancel

lauren myracle

Saturday, November 20, 10:32 PM E.S.T.

mad maddie: **dude! future hubby alert!**

SnowAngel: for real???

mad maddie: **no. cute boy, tho. very very cute.**

SnowAngel: where r u? is the wedding over?

mad maddie: **reception. boy's name = clive.**

SnowAngel: CLIVE?

mad maddie: **but i call him chive, cuz i = witty. friend of donovan.**

SnowAngel: cool—i can't wait to hear more when ur not IMing from your cell. why r u, anyway? just call me!

mad maddie: **can't. lurking behind dessert table.**

SnowAngel: maddie, get off the phone and go have fun. or else go somewhere and CALL me, cuz guess what? i think i figured out why my parents r being so weird.

mad maddie: **spill**

SnowAngel: it's zoe who helped me figure it out. she was all, "maybe what they're hiding is a GOOD thing, angela," and i think maybe she's right. i think they're buying me a car!

mad maddie: **holy shit!**

SnowAngel: i know!!! they keep talking in these hush-hush quiet voices, and then they clam up whenever i come in the room. it's extremely suspicious.

mad maddie: **well, rock on**

mad maddie: **as for me, it's bunny hop time!**

zoegirl:	maddie! ur awake and it's only 11:00! how was the wedding?
mad maddie:	**it was awesome, altho i'm kinda hungover. not terrible, tho.**
zoegirl:	tell me more
mad maddie:	**it was mainly family, so the ceremony wasn't huge, but with my family that's probably a good thing. donovan looked great in his tux, and lisa looked drop-dead gorgeous.**
zoegirl:	yeah? what was her dress like?
mad maddie:	**her dress? i don't know. it was . . . white. NOT frou-frou. for lisa it was perfect, especially cuz she's so tiny. but like, naturally tiny. healthy tiny.**
zoegirl:	did she seem happy? was she glowing? when i fall in love, it's gonna be with someone who makes me glow.
mad maddie:	**ok, excuse me while i barf**
zoegirl:	whoa, u really r hungover
mad maddie:	**uh, no, i was barfing cuz somehow ur channeling angela with this "glowing" shit. why does everyone have to get all mushy when it comes to love?**
zoegirl:	i am *not* channeling angela. u cannot compare me to angela, that is so unfair.
mad maddie:	**i don't know if lisa was glowing, but she smiled a lot, and at the reception she gave me a big hug, which surprised me. i used to think she was snobby, but now i'm wondering if she's just shy.**
mad maddie:	**she's not, like, the coolest girl in the world, but she's the coolest girl for donovan, if that makes sense. i think they're good together.**

Send   Cancel

zoegirl:	well, that's awesome. u can be cynical maddie if u have to be, but i want that someday. i wanna fall in love for real.
mad maddie:	**u don't consider mr. h for real?**
zoegirl:	don't, maddie. i don't even like to joke about that.
mad maddie:	**about what? about the fact that u almost had an affair with your horny english teacher?**
zoegirl:	i am covering my ears now. la la la.
mad maddie:	**how about his whole christianity kick, can i joke about that? ya gotta admit, it's great material. it's not very often that a guy uses God to try and lure in the girls.**
zoegirl:	please stop
mad maddie:	**zo, it happened over a year ago. it's ancient history. when WILL i be allowed to joke about it?**
zoegirl:	*never*
zoegirl:	let's change the subject. i talked to angela this morning, and she said u met some guy named after a seasoning. cilantro? paprika?
mad maddie:	**ha ha. it's clive. i just call him chive. he goes to northside.**
zoegirl:	what grade's he in?
mad maddie:	**he's a junior. he loves music, which is why he goes to n'side since they have such a good performing arts department. i told him how i wanna major in music AND advertising and then be the person who makes CD covers.**
mad maddie:	**we talked forever—he's got GORGEOUS eyes—and then we ended up macking in the corner. the moms totally caught us, which believe me was completely embarrassing.**
zoegirl:	oh god
mad maddie:	**but she was wasted 2, so she didn't care. she got all teary and started saying stuff like, "u and clive! it's meant to**

	be!" and i was like, "mom, no. i love being single." and she goes, "r u telling me ur a slut?"
zoegirl:	nuh uh
mad maddie:	**then she calls out to all my aunts and uncles in this really loud voice, "someone bring me another drink—my little girl's a slut!"**
zoegirl:	i swear, maddie, your family is so incredibly different from mine. there is no way in the world i would ever have a convo like that with my mother.
mad maddie:	**cuz your family is normal**
mad maddie:	**she was just joking, tho. she was just being wild.**
zoegirl:	was chive around for all that? did he hear your mom call u a slut?
mad maddie:	**yeah, and he laffed. that's the cool thing about him.**
zoegirl:	huh
mad maddie:	**i had FUN, zo. the whole nite was fun. i know it's not your style, but i had a blast.**
zoegirl:	so r u gonna c him again?
mad maddie:	**who, chive? i hope so, yeah, but not in a date-y way if that's what ur asking.**
zoegirl:	why not in a date-y way, if u liked him so much?
mad maddie:	**cuz i'm not looking for that. we don't all have to GLOW, zo. we really don't.**
mad maddie:	**hey, how was your first nite at Kidding Around?**
zoegirl:	i *love* it. the kids r so cute. there was this one little boy, he was maybe 3, and he had all these fake tattoos on his arm. i would point to one and say, "so what's that?" and he'd say, "a snake, but not a *real* snake." or "a bat, but not a *real* bat." or "a lightning, but not a *real*

Send   Cancel

	lightning, cuz if it was real lightning, there would be thunder. only not here. somewhere else. where the indians r."
mad maddie:	**what indians?**
zoegirl:	beats me.
zoegirl:	oh—and guess who works there with me?!
mad maddie:	**who?**
zoegirl:	doug schmidt!
mad maddie:	**doug? as in angela's doug?**
zoegirl:	well, he's not really angela's doug, seeing as how she's not the slightest bit interested. but yeah. i was like, "doug! wow!"
mad maddie:	**he's gonna be all over u, i can c it now. he's gonna use u as an inside link. cuz angela may not be interested, but it's a sure bet he's still crushing on her.**
zoegirl:	maybe. i don't know. i just think it's cool that a guy would take a job there in the 1st place.
mad maddie:	**what'd angela say when u told her?**
zoegirl:	we didn't talk about it much, cuz she was kinda distracted. she thinks her parents r buying her a car.
mad maddie:	**oh yeah, that's right—and she says U planted the idea.**
zoegirl:	i did not! i just said she shouldn't assume that whatever's going on with her parents is bad.
zoegirl:	altho i may have to revise that opinion based on a new and not-so-good development. *don't* tell angela.
mad maddie:	**don't tell angela what?**
zoegirl:	i saw her dad at starbucks this morning. i was getting cappuccinos for my parents cuz i'm such a good daughter, and there was mr. silver. and he wasn't alone.

mad maddie:	**who was he with?**
zoegirl:	a woman, wearing a tailored skirt and blouse. the kind of woman who actually uses lip liner.
mad maddie:	**lip liner, that's hardcore.**
mad maddie:	**so what r u saying?**
zoegirl:	nothing, i'm not saying anything
mad maddie:	**u don't think he's having an affair, do u???**
zoegirl:	no no no, i'm sure he's not.
zoegirl:	i just got a weird vibe, that's all.
mad maddie:	**weird how?**
zoegirl:	u know how normally mr. silver's so friendly and buddy-buddy? well, today when i went over to say hi, he looked really uncomfortable. all brusque and at the same time blushing, like he'd been caught in the act.
mad maddie:	**WHAT act?**
zoegirl:	i dunno. and he didn't introduce me to the lip liner woman, even tho she was smiling very pleasantly like "oh, and who's your little friend?" it was 1 of those moments where he *should* have introduced us, but he didn't.
zoegirl:	there was something suspicious about it. it made me worry that
zoegirl:	never mind
mad maddie:	**what?**
zoegirl:	it's stupid. it's superstitious. but like, things r going *so well* for us. ur happy, angela's happy, i'm happy. and then i think, shit, when's the bad thing gonna happen, u know?
mad maddie:	**and u think the bad thing has to do with angela's dad and the lip liner woman?**

258

zoegirl:	i didn't say that
mad maddie:	**anywayz, ur crazy. enuff bad stuff happened to us last year to last a lifetime.**
zoegirl:	tell me about it. let's c, 1st there was me and mr. h, then angela and all her boy probs, and then as if that wasn't enuff, u went all psycho with your terrible jana obsession.
mad maddie:	**"obsession"? that's a bit of an exaggeration, wouldn't u say?**
zoegirl:	no. u were like her clone. u started to talk like her, dress like her . . .
zoegirl:	i am *so* glad ur over that, btw
mad maddie:	**listen, pal. if i'm not allowed to mention mr. h, then ur not allowed to bring up jana.**
zoegirl:	fine, then u know how i feel.
zoegirl:	but don't u c the pattern? it was last year right around thanksgiving that all hell broke loose, and now here we r, right around thanksgiving again.
mad maddie:	**nooooo, zoe. it was BEFORE last thanksgiving that all hell broke loose, cuz over thanksgiving itself, we were blissing out on cumberland island. or have u forgotten?**
zoegirl:	of course i haven't forgotten!
zoegirl:	why didn't we plan a trip for this year? weren't we gonna make it a tradition?
mad maddie:	**oops, 2 late now**
zoegirl:	c! that's what's making me feel this way. we're 2 complacent, just going along like everything's fine.
mad maddie:	**yeahhhh, cuz everything IS fine.**
mad maddie:	**don't worry, zo. life is good, and ain't nothin gonna change. c ya at angela's!**

Send   Cancel

Keep reading! If you liked this book, check out these other titles.

Hell Phone
by William Sleator
0-8109-5481-8 $16.95 hardcover

This Is All:
The Pillow Book of Cordelia Kenn
by Printz Award-winner Aidan Chambers
0-8109-7060-0 $19.95 hardcover

Visit www.amuletbooks.com to download screensavers and ring tones, to find out where authors will be appearing, and to send e-cards.

Anahita's Woven Riddle
by Meghan Nuttall Sayres
0-8109-5479-6 $16.95 hardcover

Keep reading! If you liked this book, check out these other titles.

**The Chronicles of Faerie:
The Hunter's Moon**
by O.R. Melling
0-8109-9214-0 $7.95 paperback

ttyl
by Lauren Myracle
0-8109-8788-0 $6.95 paperback

ttfn
by Lauren Myracle
0-8109-5971-2 $15.95 hardcover

AVAILABLE WHEREVER BOOKS ARE SOLD

Send author fan mail to Amulet Books, Attn: Marketing, 115 West 18th Street, New York, NY 10011 or in an email to *marketing@hnabooks.com*. All mail will be forwarded. Amulet Books is an imprint of Harry N. Abrams, Inc.